# a dark
# oval
# stone

## marsena konkle

PARACLETE PRESS
Brewster, Massachusetts

A *Dark Oval Stone*
2006     First Printing

Copyright 2006 by Marsena Konkle

ISBN 1-55725-427-3

"The Charity Of Night"
Written by Bruce Cockburn
© 1997 Golden Mountain Music Corp.
Used by permission.

Library of Congress Cataloging-in-Publication Data

Konkle, Marsena.
  A dark oval stone / Marsena Konkle
  p. cm.
  ISBN 1-55725-427-3
  1. Psychological fiction.  I. Title.
PS3611.O5848D37 2006
813'.6—dc22                          2005026918

10 9 8 7 6 5 4 3 2 1

Published by Paraclete Press
Brewster, Massachusetts
www.paracletepress.com

Printed in the United States of America

$f$or Jefflee, loml.

*Wave on wave of life*

*Like the great wide ocean's roll*

*Haunting hands of memory*

*Pluck silver strands of soul*

*The damage and the dying done*

*The clarity of light*

*Gentle bows and glasses raised*

*To the charity of night*

Bruce Cockburn, "The Charity of Night"

*a* tapping noise, like a hundred small beetles striking

a windshield, woke Miriam. She buried her face in the

covers, pressing the palm of her hand against her cold nose while the rest of her body sought Paul. Instead of his radiating warmth, her feet met with cold sheets. She uncovered her head and listened. A snowplow rumbled past the house, its blade scraping against the frozen asphalt, and snow mixed with sleet beat on the window.

Miriam called Paul's name, cringing as the sound of her own voice made her temples throb. She eased out of bed and stepped over the pile of clothes she and Paul had stripped themselves of—in haste—the night before. She peered outside, her breath instantly fogging the pane, and squinted. Although it was only a little after seven and the sun was barely up, the neighborhood glimmered brightly, light magnified by the snow that was piled against the sides of houses and on driveways, spilling off tree branches and pushed into cascading lumps by the plow. Everything looked comfortably soft, yet she knew that underneath was a layer of ice, slippery and treacherous.

Paul must be running. He was crazy to be out in weather like this. One of these days he'd slip and break an arm or crack his tailbone. That had happened to a co-worker of hers once, and he had been forced to sit on a plastic, inflatable donut for six weeks. The teasing he endured, carrying that ridiculous cushion with him everywhere, was merciless. She didn't think she'd find it as funny if it happened to Paul.

The baseboards creaked, which meant Paul had turned the heat up, but it hadn't yet overcome the plunging December temperatures. Cold seeped through the window, giving Miriam goose bumps. She shivered and crawled back into bed, moving carefully so as not to jar anything loose in her body. Why on earth did she have that third martini last night? Granted, it was chocolate, and it was a Christmas party, but still . . .

She pulled the covers up to her chin, relishing the warmth of the bed in contrast to the chill of the room. Their kitten, Figment, had burrowed beneath the quilt at the end of the bed, and she snuggled her feet next to the lump he made.

"I will never have another chocolate martini as long as I live," she told Figment, her voice croaking slightly.

The phone rang, jolting her upright. She clutched her forehead, glancing at the clock. Eight fifteen. It was probably Paul's parents. They'd been calling every Saturday morning since Paul let it slip that she and Paul were trying to get pregnant. The dreaded question was always the first thing out of their mouths: "Has it happened yet?" Miriam was mightily sick of that question. Tempting as it was to let the answering machine pick up, each ring was a dagger in her head, and it had at least three more to go. She groped for the receiver.

"Hello? Yes?" She sounded more demanding and impatient than she meant to.

"Aren't you cheery this morning!" It was Esther.

"Oh, thank God. I was afraid it was my in-laws." Miriam lay back down. Esther's husband, Charles, had been Paul's roommate while they were in law school, and the Lings took credit for introducing Paul and Miriam. Of all their married friends, Esther and Charles were the only couple that both Paul and Miriam liked equally well, and the feeling seemed to be reciprocated by the Lings, whose four-year-old daughter, Mei, called them Aunt Miriam and Uncle Paul.

Esther knew Paul's parents had been hounding them for grandchildren. "You have a bun in the oven yet?" she asked in a mock elderly woman's voice.

Miriam made a strangling sound.

"So how was the party last night?" Esther wanted to know.

"We left when Claire, the new receptionist, tried to climb onto a table to demonstrate her hula dancing."

"Oh, man. I wish our office parties were that entertaining. The most I can hope for is a steak dinner from Charles's firm and a basket of cheese from my boss."

"Free food. That's something."

"Boring. I'd exchange that for the hula anytime."

"I'm sure Claire would be happy to give you lessons."

Esther snorted.

Miriam heard Paul come in and stamp snow off his feet at the back door, the sound carrying surprisingly well to their upstairs bedroom. The basement door banged as he headed downstairs to lift weights. The man had limitless energy.

"So at what point in a pregnancy," Miriam asked Esther, "do you have to actually worry about alcohol intake?"

"*Are* you pregnant?" Esther sounded surprised and not entirely happy.

"I doubt it. But I suppose, theoretically, I could be."

"Well, then, theoretically, I don't think you need to worry yet."

"I just don't want to do anything to hurt our chances. It's been a couple of months already—"

"Which is *such* a long time." Esther's voice was sharp.

"No, I know it's not." She waited for Esther to say something, and when she didn't, Miriam filled the silence. "Paul was disappointed it didn't happen right away. I'm sorry." Miriam seemed to be doing more of this lately, apologizing to her friend. "I didn't think. . . ." But the conversation was over. They hung up, and Miriam groaned.

New Year's Eve was still three weeks away, but already she had her resolutions. No alcoholic beverages with chocolate in them; be more careful of Esther's feelings.

The phone rang again, and this time Miriam did let the answering machine pick up. She needed an aspirin.

By the time she was up and trying to decide what to wear, Paul had finished exercising and was singing in the shower. Yodeling was more like it.

Clad in bra, underwear, and a pair of Paul's sunglasses, Miriam knelt in front of her dresser and unearthed from the back of the bottom drawer the sweater he had given her for her thirty-sixth birthday. She had worn it only once, to please him, before promptly burying it beneath piles of ragged t-shirts and jeans she could no longer fit into.

Miriam and Paul had been married for five years but still periodically continued their newlywed game of choosing each other's outfits when they were getting ready to go out, a ritual that amused him more than her. There was always a chance that he would be drawn to something flashy or risqué on her behalf, whereas she always had in mind his status as a young lawyer trying to make partner and therefore never asked him to wear anything more adventurous than a floral tie or polka-dotted socks. At times she sensed his disappointment in her lack of adventure, but she comforted herself with the thought that she had his best interests at heart.

Paul had mentioned the Tango sweater, as he called it, the night before as he was rooting through her stacks of sweaters, wanting to dress her for the party. She had ignored him, but now, in a moment of guilty weakness, because he really seemed to like the sweater, she felt compelled to get it out.

Yet: If he saw it, he'd be sure to make her wear it to the mall, and she didn't feel up to standing out in a crowd. Paul emerged from the bathroom with a towel wrapped around his waist. Too late, she stuffed the sweater in and slammed the drawer, trying frantically to hide the yellow fluff that stuck out.

With a triumphant cry, Paul leapt toward her. "So you didn't throw it away, you little liar," he said, a grin showing all his teeth as he tried to reach around her.

"I never said I did," she retorted, blocking his way.

They scuffled for a moment, with him scrambling for the drawer and her batting his hands away until he changed tactics, grabbing her under the arms to drag her toward the middle of the room, her five-foot-five frame no match for his six-foot, athletic body. She twisted, trying not to laugh because she knew from past experience that if she started giggling, she'd have even less chance of fending him off, and thrust her feet against the dresser. The sunglasses, which were too big for her, fell off her head, and Paul nearly crunched them under a knee. He forced her arms together so he could grasp both her wrists in one hand as he reached for the drawer with the other.

Paul briefly loosened his grip on her wrists in order to sit on her and she seized the opportunity to yank the towel from his waist and move her knee dangerously close to his crotch. When he yelped and moved to protect himself, she wrapped her arms around his neck and tried to knock him over. But in vain. He flipped her up and onto the bed as if she weighed nothing, just barely missing the spot where Figment was still napping, or more likely hiding from their noise. Paul straddled her with a self-satisfied grin on his face, his hands immobilizing her shoulders.

"I don't suppose you'd be so kind as to give me back those sunglasses," she said, squinting up at him.

"You realize, don't you," he said, kissing first one eyelid and then the other, "that you no longer have a choice."

She sighed, accepting as a consequence of her defeat having to wear the sweater to the mall. "I really wanted to skip the whole Christmas present thing this year."

Paul kissed her, lingering and shifting his position so she could feel how aroused he was. What did she expect, starting a wrestling match in her underwear? They'd never get the shopping done at this rate.

"They're probably selling the very last Christmas tree as we speak," she protested.

"Who needs a tree?"

"The shelves at Toys-'Я-Us are being cleared at this very moment. I heard on the news there's a shortage of toys."

"Mei will be sad. But we'll be so happy."

Miriam returned his kiss. Amazing, how ridiculously easy it was to ensure Paul's happiness. If only a little sex could do the same for her. She thought at first to let it simply be a quickie, to get it over with, but he resisted when she tried to turn him onto his back so she could be on top. He wanted to play. She allowed him to coax her into forgetting her headache and her self-consciousness, willed herself to relax under his fingertips, which sought to pleasure her first. It was a rare forgetting, not only because of her tightly bound self, but because their love-making had been utilitarian as of late, enjoyment and spontaneity replaced by the demands of her irregular cycle and Paul's desire to have a child.

*Ah, yes,* she thought, with a sharp intake of breath. *Here we are.*


Paul was grinding coffee beans when she joined him in the kitchen. He had suggested that a little food would do her good before they faced the holiday crowds. She put two slices of raisin bread in the toaster and dug in the refrigerator for orange juice. They had both dozed for a while after making love and now it was nearly lunchtime.

"So what did Bob say last night?" Paul asked around a bite of toast. He leaned against the counter, waiting for more toast to pop up while she settled on the other side of the island, facing him and cautiously sipping her juice.

"About what?" she evaded, knowing full well what he was referring to. She had hoped he wouldn't ask. Bob Carley was her boss, the owner of the architectural firm, and Paul had been trying to convince her for months to show him some of her own sketches. The thought of doing so turned her stomach. Paul had made a valiant effort the night before at the party—and it had nearly worked—by challenging her to a bet. If Carley, as she always thought of him, loosened his tie, Paul had said, she would have to talk to him about her portfolio. Just ask him to look at it and give her some pointers. If the tie stayed tight, she could shake his hand at the end of the night and tell him that she'd see him at the office on Monday when she'd be opening his mail and answering his phone, per usual.

The only reason she had agreed to the bet in the first place was because she had been so certain Carley would not loosen his tie. Miriam had been with the company for six years, and in all that time, when he required that she work late with him, on Saturdays, at parties, even at the summer picnic, for heaven's sake, she had never seen him without a carefully knotted tie. He'd take off his jacket and roll up his sleeves, but that was as casual as he ever got. Agreeing to the bet had seemed a safe way to please Paul, to make him think she was willing to ask for Carley's feedback on her designs.

"Seriously, Miriam, what did he say?"

"Couldn't you tell from my expression?" She didn't want to lie to Paul, but she hated even more to disappoint him. At the party he had watched from across the room as she chatted innocently with Carley about one of their newest clients, who was renovating an old house in the historic district of Barrington, a northwest suburb of Chicago.

Why had he taken his tie off halfway through the party, she wondered, stuffing it carelessly into his back pocket? It was so unlike him. Suddenly it occurred to her to be suspicious.

"Hey. Wait a minute." She pushed her plate of toast away and noted that Paul immediately looked sheepish, as if he could tell she had just caught on. "Why did you make the bet about his tie? Did you know something I didn't?"

"The point is, you didn't keep up your end of the bargain, did you? Come on, you can admit it."

"Don't sidestep my question. Did you bribe him or something?"

"Of course not. Whatever gave you that idea?" He shrugged, still not meeting her eyes.

"You are such a rat," she said, throwing a crust at him.

Paul brushed crumbs off his shirt and busied himself with petting Figment, who had jumped onto the counter next to him. The cat stretched under Paul's hand before catapulting back to the floor and fleeing the room as if his tail were on fire.

"And he's off!" Paul yelled down the hallway after him.

"Maybe you should do a little penance and shovel Mrs. Harmel's sidewalk. Before shopping."

"I gave you an orgasm this morning, isn't that penance enough?"

"I consider that a reward you didn't deserve."

Paul leaned over the counter to kiss her, and she smiled against his lips. "You'd be so bored without me," he said.

"Go shovel," she answered. "We've got a lot to do today."

# two

*M*iriam curled up on the couch and closed her eyes.
Maybe if she held very still for a few more minutes, she'd be
able to shake the last remnants of her headache. She could
vaguely hear the metallic scratch of Paul's shovel against
the pavement as he worked his way down their driveway,
no doubt formulating more reasons why he should have a
snow blower. For years she had resisted his getting one; the
expense seemed frivolous when the machine would be
needed only a few times each winter. Recently, though, she
had decided to buy him one for Christmas. Perhaps it would
ease a source of conflict between them: their neighbor, Mrs.
Harmel.

Mrs. Harmel was eighty-four and a widow, but in the winter, whenever Miriam suggested that Paul shovel her sidewalk, or in the fall, when the gutters needed cleaning, Paul reminded her impatiently that Mrs. Harmel paid a neighbor boy to do such chores.

"But we don't know how much money she has," Miriam had pointed out on several occasions. "Maybe she can't really afford it."

"That's not our business," Paul replied. "Plus," he'd argued, "is it right for us to take money away from the boy, who, thank heavens, is doing something more productive than watching television or playing video games all day? Mrs. Harmel is not your mother, nor is she your ticket out of purgatory."

Months later, this comment still had the power to sting.

Like Mrs. Harmel, Miriam's mother had been widowed and alone for many years, paying neighborhood youths to put up the storm windows, cut the grass, set traps for mice in the basement. But when Miriam's sister, Theresa, or her brother, Steven, offered any help, she stubbornly turned back to whatever food she was preparing—she spent most of her time in the kitchen—offended and indignant. They all knew she didn't have the money to spend, but she wouldn't hear of letting them do any of the work for her.

Her eyes still closed, Miriam heard a neighbor's snow blower start up across the street, its roar muffled and distant, but still loud enough to obliterate the sound of Paul's shovel. He was taking his time, being especially diligent about removing the treacherous layer of ice. Just like Paul.

Miriam opened her eyes and stared at the ceiling, braving a painful moment of memory and reflection. Theresa's conversations with their mother always turned into one-sided harangues about going to the doctor, moving into a nursing home, giving up her driver's license. At least seven years before her death, their mother began hanging up on Theresa when she called and refusing to open the door if Theresa stopped by, once even threatening through the screen door to call the police if she didn't go away. Miriam's sister gave up after that incident, avenging herself by appearing at only one family gathering per year, a self-righteous tilt to her posture.

It had fallen to Miriam to provide care for her aging mother. Miriam gave up her apartment and, claiming financial difficulties, moved back home, enduring stoically her mother's weekly lectures about needing to grow up and take responsibility for her life and budget. "No man wants a woman who isn't smart enough to balance her own checkbook."

Still, her mother had been the one in the neighborhood and at the local parish who could be counted on for meals whenever there was a delivery or death: The Two Ds, as Steven put it. Miriam helped with the cooking and accompanied her mother to the needy person's home as a way of allowing her to stay active while also keeping her from getting behind the wheel of a car. She also made a big deal of Mother's Day and birthdays so she could spring clean or plant flowers as a gift rather than an act of unwanted charity. It was exhausting, to care for her mother within such a system of subterfuge, and when her mother died the year before Miriam met Paul, Miriam told herself it was probably for the best.

Down the street, the snow blower switched off, and Miriam realized she couldn't hear Paul's shovel anymore. He must've finished, so they could finally get going. She pulled herself off the couch and started clearing the dishes on the kitchen counter while she waited for him to come in. Out of nowhere two sets of claws attached themselves to her calf. She yelped, and Figment pranced out of the room, his tail twitching. Pulling up her jeans, she could see red, needle-thin welts appearing. "Dumb cat," she yelled after him.

There was a knock at the front door. Immediately she envisioned Paul, armed with a large scoop of fresh snow, standing aimed and ready to throw. She took her time answering. But when she opened the door, she found instead the diminutive Mrs. Harmel standing on the stoop in a pink quilted robe and slippers with snow mounded on the open toes. Her filmy eyes were wide, peering over her reading glasses, and when Miriam told her, confusedly, to come in, she just stood staring, her thin lips quivering. She was a small woman, impossibly frail, with tightly permed hair and dark veins lining the tops of her bony hands.

"What is it?" Miriam asked, and the old woman reached past the doorjamb, grasped her sleeve and pulled with surprising strength. In front of Mrs. Harmel's house, right next door, a figure lay motionless on the sidewalk.

Miriam's confused mind catalogued what Paul had been wearing: red sweat pants, green windbreaker over a gray sweatshirt. Blue snow boots with the fuzzy white lining peeking over the top. His feet were splayed wide, pointing in opposite directions as if they had simultaneously come loose at the ankle and toppled sideways.

Miriam plowed through the snow. CPR. There was a shovel under his back, the wooden handle sticking out like an unusable limb. She had to dredge up memories of first-aid from junior high health class. *Oh, please.* She compressed his chest, pressed her mouth to his in a way she had never done before, praying with each shuddering breath.

"Don't move him." Mrs. Harmel's voice, distant, as though piercing through a fog. "I called an ambulance already."

She flashed hot and cold; the nerves in her hands registered with clarity the slickness of Paul's windbreaker and the slight give in his chest when she pushed down. She heard nothing but her own gasping. The ambulance siren burst into her awareness only when someone moved her forcibly away, and even then her arms wanted to keep pumping, her mouth to keep seeking his.

She couldn't tell how long she and her husband were on that sidewalk together. Is it possible to black out without losing consciousness? She was in the back of the ambulance, clutching Paul's boot. *How did they get to his bare skin so quickly?* she wondered through the screaming of the siren.

The emergency room had orange chairs with torn vinyl. *We need to go home now because he's only thirty-nine.*
But the nurses merely ushered her back to the chair and into a new way of keeping time, of understanding. The

present was rendered meaningless, and the past and future were christened Before and After.

Paul was gone.

Her mind emptied of everything except her mother. How she would have excelled in this emergency, her body swelling with a grief to overwhelm Miriam's. She thought back to the sons her mother had lost, two of Miriam's brothers, one dead before Miriam was born and the other killed in a school fire. The constancy of her mother's weeping reprimanded her as she sat picking fuzz off her yellow sweater, unable to shed a tear. Even her breath was raspy dry. She tried to remember how to pray, but couldn't think of a single useful word.

It was her mother who first planted in Miriam the idea that although death is certainly inevitable, it might be possible to walk with an eye toward heaven so that when the inevitable begins to pour down, she might be ready with an umbrella or by a quick dash might reach a place of safety. For as often as her mother whispered her own prayers of deliverance and help, she would entreat: *Pray, Miriam, pray. Recite your prayers often so you will be spared. So you won't know the pain I have.* And so Miriam tried to say her prayers, fueled by the fear of what could happen.

*The fear of what could happen.* Without warning, her attention snapped back to the present. *Myocardial infarction. Heart attack.* Miriam's mind stuck like a broken record. *Fatal. Heart attack.* It couldn't happen. Paul was only thirty-nine.

In those first days of silence, when Job could do nothing but sit on an ash heap with his clothes torn, scraping his sores with a bit of broken pottery, did he think dully, "I would have bargained with You." *I would have given anything. Everything.* But even those words were brittle autumn leaves—vacant crisps of their former selves.

A hand on her arm, a piece of paper, a clipboard. "We need to release your husband's body to the coroner. He will confirm the cause of death."

She looked up blankly.

"All unexpected deaths require an autopsy," the orderly explained, walking to a door and motioning for her to follow. "Would you like to see him?"

Miriam stepped into a room without sound—devoid of beeps or clicks or voices.

*So this is what he will look like when he's dead.*

A sheet lay crumpled at the foot of Paul's bed; she took a few steps and picked it up with both hands, held it up, twisted it right then left, examined it for evidence. The sheet was white and clean except for a dusty shoe print where someone had stepped on it. No blood. She looked at Paul's still body, then at the sheet in her hands. *There's been a mistake.*

He was covered up to his neck with a second sheet, and she stumbled forward, the sheet she held tangling around her feet. He never slept this way—had to have an arm slung on top of the covers, even in winter when his skin would goose pimple and ache with cold. His claustrophobia was a secret she had cradled in her hands like an egg with a thin shell, so small and delicate it existed in a realm of its own, beyond any jokes or teasing banter.

She peeled back the sheet covering Paul, and her knuckles brushed against his chest, felt the cold skin that had already lost its right to be called skin, that couldn't be his, couldn't be anyone's. Grasping his forearm with one hand, she willed him to tighten his bicep into a rock, to impress her, to show off. To simply move. She squeezed his arm rhythmically, in, out, in, out. His face looked like wax, his lips so pale they blended into his cheeks.

"Miriam?"

She clasped her hands at her chest and swiveled toward the door.

"Do you have family to call?" the male nurse asked.

She stared at a streak of gray hair at his temples.

"C'mon. I'll show you to the lounge." He placed his hand against Miriam's back, the gentle and steady pressure of a dancer leading his partner through a turn at the end of the dance floor. With his free hand the nurse tried to take the sheet out of her fists. He tugged several times before she let go, staring at her open hands. They were dirty from her fall on the sidewalk where Paul lay. She tucked her palms under her arms and let herself be pushed toward the lounge, where she sank into a battered, Aztec-patterned couch. On beige walls hung framed prints of azaleas and cottages by a beach, scenes that made no sense to her. She wondered who she should call. Her mother was dead. Esther and Charles were out of town, visiting Charles's parents for the rest of the weekend. Her brother, Steven. Of course.

Miriam's stomach purged itself of raisin toast, coffee, all memory of chocolate martinis, the monstrous hope that this was all a dream. She was grateful for the way her eyes burned.

"Darling, your face is dirty," whispered Steven.

When she finally looked up and saw her brother kneeling on the tile floor with her, she felt pain—a sharp intake of breath—not for herself, but for him. Because she saw that he knew from experience what it felt to be her. At this exact moment in time. In his eyes was an awareness of suffering that caused her to despair. He pushed her hair over her shoulders, kissed her forehead.

Miriam looked over his shoulder at the cubbyhole where a nurse could reach through the wall and retrieve cups of bodily fluids left by patients. It was fitting that her face was dirty. Ashes in place of tears. "I'll wash when I cry," she said.

Steven's hands moved to her shoulders and she felt the pressure of his thumbs. "You *will* cry," he said fiercely.

How had he known that's what she meant?

"Right now, you respond however you need to." He shook her a little, his eyes intent on hers.

"But Mom . . ." she whispered.

"Our Lady of Perpetual Tears? Hers is not the only way to grieve."

**three**

*t*he bench seat in Steven's truck creaked with cold when Miriam got in. The windows were covered with snow, making the interior shadowy and dark. With wide sweeps of his scraper, Steven created swaths for light to push through, chipping away at the layer of ice that had formed on the windshield. Miriam followed his movements with her eyes, shivering as cold air poured out of the heat vents. Neither of them spoke during the drive home.

At the front door of her house she fumbled for her keys, distracted by the red-handled shovel leaning against the railing; Steven reached out to help, discovering the door was unlocked. While he hung up his coat, Miriam hurried up the stairs to the bedroom, tossing her purse onto the unmade bed and flinging open the door of her closet. On the top shelf were boxes she hadn't opened in years, but she believed her mother's rosary to be in one of them.

The first box, so heavy she could hardly get it down without dropping it, was from high school, filled with notes given to her by friends as they passed each other in the hallway between classes, the tassel from her graduation cap, medals from swim meets, yearbooks. She shoved it aside and reached for another. This one held more promise. Odds and ends from her mother's home. Scarves, piles of plastic bead necklaces every color of the rainbow, and dickies—the faux turtlenecks that women of a previous generation wore under sweaters when all they wanted was the color of the folded neck without the warmth or bulk of an actual shirt.

She turned the box over and rummaged through the pile on the floor. She longed to hold the rosary, worn smooth by her mother over the course of many years, longed to press it against her chest until it left dimpled indentations on her skin, to feel each individual bead between her fingers so she could remember one of the many prayers she had learned while growing up. Her mother had never been at a loss for words.

"Miriam?" Steven peered into the bedroom. "I made some tea." He stepped around the piles and handed her a steaming mug. Chamomile, she could smell, which inexplicably turned her stomach. She pretended to take a sip and set the cup on the floor.

Steven sat at the foot of the bed. "Anything I can help with?" he asked, inclining his head toward the mess on the floor.

She shook her head, carelessly pulling down another box and spilling its contents.

"What about phone calls? You want me to make some for you?"

She froze, an empty box dangling from her hand, junk cluttered around her ankles. Whether he meant it or not, she felt his suggestion as a slap. "Right," she said, blinking. "Right. I should call people. I'll do that now." She dropped the box, only momentarily wondering if she should take the time to clean up.

On her way past Steven, he said, "Get the hardest one over with first."

She stopped at the doorway and looked back at him. "Which one is that?"

"Paul's parents."

"Oh. Okay."

In her address book by the kitchen phone, she looked up the number for Paul's parents and dialed with shaking fingers, pushing the wrong buttons several times and having to start over again. The holes in the receiver bit into her ear, and there was an eternity of echoing silence between rings. When Henry answered, she had the phone pressed so hard against her head that his voice exploded in her ear. Momentarily, she was unable to speak.

"I said hello," he repeated. "Who is this?"

"Dad," she said, the word sticking slightly, as it always did. "It's me."

"Miriam. You wouldn't believe the crank calls we've been getting this week. I can't prove it yet, but I know it's those damn teenagers next door, you know, the ones who—"

"Is Mom there?" Miriam interrupted. "I've got news that I don't—"

"Martha," Henry yelled without covering the phone. "Get on the other line, Miriam's got news!"

*Oh, God,* Miriam thought, her heart beating somewhere in the vicinity of her toes. *He thinks I'm pregnant.*

There was a click and the fumbling of a second extension.

"Son?" Henry inquired, expecting Paul to be on the phone, too, which was a fair assumption. Often all four of them talked together so nothing had to be repeated. "Is Paul on the line?"

"No," Miriam said. "Actually, it's about him."

There was a silence in which Miriam half expected them to guess or ask questions, but when they did neither, she continued. "We had a snow storm last night, about nine inches, and he was out shoveling. Actually, he went running this morning before he shoveled, which makes it even harder to understand because he was in such great shape—"

"What on earth are you babbling about?" Henry demanded.

"He's gone."

"Gone? What do you mean, gone?" Their minds did not transition quickly from pregnancy to death.

"Gone," she repeated.

"He left you." It was not a question.

The accusation gave her the incentive to spit it out. "He had a heart attack. Myocardial something or other. He was dead before we got to the hospital." She cringed. Maybe that was more blunt than necessary.

Neither of them said anything. She could hear them both breathing heavily into their separate extensions and was unnerved by their lack of response. *Do something,* she pleaded inwardly, whether to herself or them or God, she didn't know. She stared across the island into the family room where Steven now waited so patiently for her, Paul's latest *Sports Illustrated* draped over his knees. Paul's sweatshirt was on the floor next to the couch where he had dropped it after his run. She was forever picking up his trail of sweaty clothes, an annoyance she had been so damn sure she could live without.

Still, Henry and Martha said nothing.

On the kitchen side of the island where she leaned was another, lower counter, out of sight to anyone in the family room, a natural place for bills, unanswered letters, keys, library books, the phone. The plastic bag of personal effects she had brought home from the hospital.

"Is this . . . ?" Martha spoke for the first time. "Are you, I mean? You're not serious. Are you?" Her voice dissolved and then rose in a high keen.

"That's enough, Martha," Henry snapped. "Say good-bye now." He waited until her line clicked obediently off and her cries receded to the background. "We'll be on the first flight tomorrow morning. I'll let you know when to pick us up at the airport. In the meantime, don't make any arrangements, because I'll take care of everything once I get there, you hear me?"

Miriam didn't respond. She wondered what, exactly, he meant.

"You hear me?" he pressed. "Don't do anything."

"Okay, yes."

He hung up, apparently satisfied.

She placed the phone on its stand and gave a strangled laugh. Steven looked up from the magazine he had been staring at, which she knew he had absolutely zero interest in. "He told me not to do anything without him."

She dialed Esther's cell phone by heart and left a message. The Lings were visiting Charles's parents in Green Bay, Wisconsin, and since she and Esther had talked that morning, they wouldn't be expecting to hear from her. She left a message, asking them to call back, and knew that without her stating it, Esther would be able to hear the disaster in her voice.

She called Carley, and then Paul's boss, his sports buddies, their friends, and a few co-workers, amazed by the calmness with which she delivered the news. Paul had died that morning and they could watch the paper for details about the funeral. No, she didn't need anything right now, thank you. After each call, she was equally glad that it was over and that she had remembered to thank them.

She put off the conversation with Theresa until last, sitting down at the island while she explained what happened, in detail, parrying as many of her sister's questions as she could.

"I'll be there in half an hour," Theresa said, finally.

"Thanks, but there's really nothing to do—"

"There's no question about it. I should be there."

"No, really, I'm fine. Steven's here—"

"Oh, since Steven's there, you don't need me? Was he at the hospital with you, too?"

"No, it's not that. I do need you, it's just that I'm not exactly sure what needs to be done yet."

"Have you called your priest?"

"Yes. I'm meeting with Father Jake tomorrow about the funeral."

"What about the funeral luncheon?"

"What about it?"

"Well, for starters, where are you having it?"

"I don't know. The parish hall, I guess."

"You can't be serious."

"Why?" Miriam was confused. "I've been to funerals there and they do a nice job. Plus, we know most of the people there and the women will help—"

"Right. The little old gossips with nothing better to do than stick marshmallows in Jell-O and call it salad. Yuck. I'll do it myself."

"You will?"

Theresa apparently took that as an agreement, and Miriam didn't try to dissuade her. Theresa was happiest, and by extension, the whole family was happiest, when she was in control of something.

"It'll have to be at my house," Theresa declared, "so I can do it right. I'll draw up a map and we'll bring copies to the funeral. I'll need to rent a few chairs. . . ." her voice trailed off. "If anyone wants to bring food, tell them no. Especially if they have blue hair and look like the sort who put grated carrot and coconut in lime Jell-O. . . ."

Miriam swiveled in her chair and rolled her eyes at Steven. He held up his hands in sympathy.

Finally, Theresa said, "I've got to tell Carl. I'll call you later."

Hanging up the phone, Miriam settled back on her chair and rested her head on her hand. She wondered how Theresa's husband, Carl, would take the news, then thought of their son, Ben, who was close to Paul and spent as much time at their house as he could—not only, Miriam thought, because he loved beating Paul at video games, but to get some distance from Theresa.

She turned to look at Steven. "I should let Theresa call Ben, right? That's her job, as his mother."

Steven brought his mug to the kitchen sink and dribbled some dish soap into it.

"It would be interfering for me to call him while she's busy telling Carl."

Steven dried his hand on his jeans and used a fingertip to push the phone toward her.

She dialed with a sense of urgency. "Please answer," she muttered, listening impatiently to the rings. He was usually pretty quick to pick up, unless it was morning or he was in class, neither of which would be true now, at dinnertime on a Saturday. Just as she was about to give up, Ben answered. Above the hiss of the phone, she could hear the noise of a crowd. She had to raise her voice to be heard, which felt wrong, as she told him about Paul.

"Oh, my God," he exclaimed several times. Stunned.

"I'm coming home tonight," he said, finally. "There's a bus that leaves from the student union in an hour, and if I hurry I can still catch it."

"You don't need to do that. I'm sure your dad will pick you up tomorrow if you want him to."

"I don't want to wait until tomorrow."

"The funeral won't be for a few days. . . ."

"You don't want me there?" he said quietly. The plaintiveness of his voice made him seem so much younger than a junior in college, bringing to mind his sweet, three-year-old little face pressed nose to nose with hers as he tried to master the art of Eskimo kisses.

"No, it's not that." Miriam paused, wanting to comfort him somehow. "I could come get you tonight," she offered, fearing as she did so that he would take her up on it. How on earth would she explain this to Theresa?

"No, that's okay. I'll take the bus. I've done it before. Hold on," he said.

Miriam waited.

"My mom's calling. Can I call you when I know what time I'll arrive? Can I stay at your place? Will it be too late?"

"No, I mean yes. Call me. That'll be fine."

She hung up, feeling queasy, and buried her head in her arms. "I think I just screwed up," she said. "Theresa's going to kill me when she finds out I called Ben before she had a chance."

Steven shrugged. "Maybe she'll surprise you."

She groaned. "And maybe hell will freeze over."

"I'm sure Ben was glad to hear it from you."

Yes, she agreed. She'd think about him, not Theresa.

"Let's go get something to eat," Steven suggested. "How's Chinese sound?" His gentle touch on her shoulder helped her up and out of the house to the restaurant, where she tried valiantly to eat something. Steven wielded his chopsticks with a flourish, picking single kernels of rice off her plate. He talked about his upholstery business, seeming to know that she welcomed his voice, even if she didn't welcome conversation, exactly.

She watched him as he talked. The way his short hair, which was thick but almost completely gray, showed the contours of his scalp. His brown eyes—not as dark as hers—were shadowed by his heavy forehead. Most of all, she loved his hands, the stubby fingers that took such a beating in order to create beauty, transforming furniture left on the side of the road or found in resale shops into works of art.

"You've always taken such good care of me," she blurted. He paused, mid-bite, to smile at her, and she looked away from his gaze. Then she stabbed a piece of broccoli with a chopstick and twirled it.

It was Steven, home from college for Christmas break, who told Miriam, when she was a curious six-year-old, the briefest, most essential facts surrounding the death of their oldest brother, trying to explain that he had lived and then was gone before she was born. He allowed her to slip a picture of Edwin, Jr., which had been taken in his uniform before he went overseas, out of its protective pocket in the photo album and touch it. He watched without comment or warning as she smudged the glossy finish, trying to imagine how stubbly his shorn hair must have felt. Even at that age, she understood grief to be the defining quality of both her parents' lives, a sadness for which she would never be able to atone. When she was nine, Vincent, who was only a year older than she, whom she had imitated and idolized and fought with, died, too. The repeat tragedy, the impact it had on her, would have been unbearable if not for Steven. She nibbled the broccoli and wrinkled her nose before pushing her plate away.

It was nearly midnight when Steven left to get Ben from the bus station. She found several reasons to go into the kitchen, taking a dirty glass to the sink, restacking the mail on the counter, even looking in the fridge, when really all she wanted was to be near the phone in case Esther rang.

A noise by the back door startled Miriam, and she instinctively ducked behind the counter, suddenly aware of how easy it would be for someone to see her through the curtainless windows. Her heart knocked against her knees. Over the sound of her breathing, she heard the noise again. Figment! Still crouching, she scrambled out of the kitchen to the back door. The lock scraped and resisted, but when she finally opened the door a crack, Figment burst in, crying pathetically. He looked more like a rat than a kitten, his fur wet and slick against his body, eyes bulging beneath enormous ears. She made sure the lock was secure before scooping him up. "Kitty," she whispered, curling up on the couch with Figment cradled against her stomach. "How on earth did you get outside?" Guilty for not noticing his absence, she held his tail so he could lick the tip of it, feeling the damp chill of his body seep into her belly. His tongue periodically scraped her fingers.

When Figment had warmed himself sufficiently to seek out his food dish, Miriam braced her feet against the coffee table—a monstrously heavy antique with squat pedestal legs and iron accents—and pushed it away from the couch, scooting along on her butt, pushing with her feet until it was against the far wall. In the empty space on the floor, she had room to gather from all corners of the house photo albums, framed pictures, and shoe boxes filled with loose and forgotten snapshots. While she waited for Steven to get back with Ben, she would start putting together a collage to show at the wake.

Figment happily scrabbled his front paws under a pile of photos, scattering them across the carpet.

One of Paul's baseball buddies was a photography enthusiast. Even in the middle of a tournament, Kevin's camera was never far from him. He had taken a picture of Miriam and Paul the summer before, and even now, she couldn't decide if she hated or loved it. Paul was standing in front of the batter's fence, feet crossed, legs magnificently outlined by blue tights, a bat over his shoulder and his free hand grasping the chain links near where Miriam stood on the other side of the fence. His expression was intense beneath the curved brim of his baseball cap, grim pleasure over the feel of the bat in his hand and its thin weight resting on his shoulder and, she imagined, grim exasperation over her.

"But don't you think you'd enjoy coaching a Little League team?" she had asked in the car on the way to the park. She had to speak loudly over the wind noise since they were in Paul's silver Miata, or his mid-life crisis warm-up, as she had affectionately named it.

"I don't have time. You know that."

"You've got time to play for the Chicago Laws."

"Yes, and you complain about that." He shifted gears abruptly, made a tight turn. "What is this really about? You want me to quit the team?"

"No, of course not. I just don't understand why teaching kids to play the game would take the pleasure of it from you."

He pulled into a parking spot and turned the car off, gripping the steering wheel. Over the windshield, they could see guys warming up, stretching, calling to each other, hear the crack of bat against ball, the noise of summer. "I do not need to be reformed by you," he said, getting out of the car and slamming the door. Glove tucked under his arm, he trotted toward his teammates, leaving Miriam swimming in misery in the passenger seat.

He was right. He didn't need to change. She didn't really know what compelled her to push Paul into doing things he didn't want to do.

Kevin had taken the picture of them between innings, while they were waiting for the visiting team to move onto the field. Miriam stood against the batter's fence, her hands raised to shoulder height, fingers jabbed through the chain links, eyes squinting into the sun, the diamond-shaped holes casting gray shadows across her face. Paul's free arm stretched above her, and she wished now, as she had then, that she could apologize.

She placed the photo in a pile with a few others she had already chosen. A few wedding photos. Paul and Charles in their caps and gowns with purple hoods, graduating from law school. Thick glasses, hair like a pile of bright straw, striped shirt and enormous triangular collar from junior high. Tee ball in his parents' backyard, the wood bat top-heavy and nearly as big as he; he had refused, at four years old, to even look at the balloon-like plastic red bat his mother had wanted him to play with. A baby in the kitchen sink, water splashing, gumming the porcelain.

Miriam flipped on the television. A World War II documentary on the History Channel flickered blue against the blank windows. Figment, now warm and dry, pranced across the floor—he loved to prance, sometimes turning his body sideways and scuttling on his tiptoes—swatting her outstretched feet as he went by. She wiggled her toes for him, regretting it when he sunk his sharp claws into them.

The stiff photo album pages creaked slightly as she turned them. Birthday parties, Christmas at Paul's parents' home in Michigan, barbeques in the backyard, a trip they had taken with the Lings to Kentucky to celebrate Charles's promotion to junior partner and her and Paul's first wedding anniversary. Nothing stood out to her.

Until the very last picture, which caused her momentarily to stop breathing. She and Paul had taken kayak lessons together, wanting to learn how to navigate river rapids. Their instructor had snapped the photo while standing at the edge of the dock, zooming in on the moment when Miriam finally mastered the trick of flipping upside down and righting herself in one swift motion. Her eyes were closed, hands lofting the paddle high, head thrown back with the unexpected synergy between body and kayak and water. Paul's expression, in his own kayak, eyes locked on her face, was naked with joy, the physical manifestation of love and unadulterated good fortune. She had not taken in his expression before, had not dreamed of being the recipient of such a look.

She was still staring at his face when the doorbell rang, bringing her instantly to her feet, heart pounding. Figment disappeared under the couch. The History Channel droned about the German blitz on London. The doorbell rang again, three, four times, in a pattern she thought she should know. Steven wouldn't ring the bell—he had a key. On her way down the hall, she stumbled over a pair of Paul's shoes.

"Miriam?" The voice. Recognition made her throat tight.

Esther stood on the porch, the limp form of her sleeping four-year-old daughter draped over her shoulder. "I called this afternoon and you were in the bathroom and I made Steven tell me. I made him. But now," she shifted Mei in her arms. "I don't know what to do."

A plow rumbled past in a fury of flashing lights, warring with the snow that wouldn't quit. Esther stepped into the house, the storm door squeaking behind her. She slipped out of her snowy shoes and headed for the couch, where she put

Mei down, pulling a blanket off a nearby chair to tuck around the tiny body. Miriam watched silently, still standing beside the open door. Esther shut it and faced her.

"Do you have stuff to bring in?" Miriam asked in a whisper.

"Oh, Miriam." The quiver in Esther's voice thrummed like a rubber band against Miriam's skin.

Arms wrapped around her friend, Miriam coveted the release she imagined Esther must feel as she sobbed.

# four

*W*hen Miriam awoke the next morning, she was surprised to find herself on the pullout couch with Esther.

Reaching out a hand, she fingered her friend's silky pajamas, trying to recall the crisis Esther was having that would have meant letting Paul sleep alone all night.

Lazily, but in less time than it took to blink, she imagined the pleasure of sneaking upstairs and crawling into bed with him, then: the sidewalk! Where snow had melted under her knees and everything had changed. Ruthlessly, she pressed knuckles into her bruised hip, willing her eyes to tear, ashamed that she had for a second forgotten.

Here she was, with Esther in the family room; Mei was on the living room couch, Steven was in her bed, Ben was in the guest bedroom. How could she have forgotten?

She should say her prayers. Couldn't think of a single one. Maybe this morning, before Henry and Martha arrived, she'd have time to find her mother's rosary.

Movement caught her eye; Mei was tiptoeing to Esther's side of the bed. The little girl had on a pink nightgown that flowed with ruffles and purple pansies, a strong contrast to the black hair that framed her face in a blunt bob. "She's probably going to be a cheerleader," Esther had once said, despairingly, as Mei flounced and twirled around the room. Esther was herself a beautiful woman, tall and slender with smooth skin, long hair she constantly fought to keep behind her ears, and golden brown eyes that were unusually wide, given her Chinese parents. But those eyes snapped with defiance and dared anyone to mistake her beauty for weakness.

Mei put her mouth against Esther's ear and whispered, "Ma?"

Miriam considered distracting Mei and letting Esther sleep, but to move her arms and legs required an act of will, a conscious decision that took too much effort.

Mei jiggled the mattress beside her mother's face. "Ma!"

Esther jolted awake. "Shhhh, honey, Miriam's sleeping."

"No, I'm awake."

They both pushed themselves up into a sitting position.

"I haven't used an alarm clock in four years," Esther groaned, touching her swollen eyelids with the tips of her fingers.

"I'm four," Mei announced.

"Yes, and there's a direct correlation between the two."

"What did she say?" Mei asked Miriam.

Figment chose that moment to jump onto the bed with them, and Mei, who had not seen the kitten before, squealed. The cat launched himself out of the room, with Mei in fast pursuit.

"Hey, watch it," Esther called after Mei, who didn't slow down. "Your cat will need a shrink after our visit. We'll pay for half."

"At least it'll keep Mei out of the basement," Miriam said.

Several times they had discovered the girl, though not yet tall enough to switch on the lights, alone in the dark basement, fingering Paul's chisels or trying to hammer nails into his workbench by the glimmer of a night-light.

"Paul still hasn't put a lock on that door," Miriam apologized, thinking of the list on the inside of the kitchen cabinet where household needs were itemized and crossed off in accordance with a set of priorities different from her own. "Build shelves for the kayaks," for instance, could have waited until after the house was made safe for Mei. Suddenly, it occurred to her what she had said. "He never will put a lock on that door," she corrected.

Mei crawled onto the bed, purring like a cat and nuzzling Esther. "Hey. Where's Uncle Paul?" she suddenly wanted to know.

Miriam blanched, not knowing whether to answer her, look to Esther for guidance, or simply throw up. Theresa was fond of telling her that throwing up was not a good coping mechanism, but sometimes it seemed the best option. The phone rang and she got up to answer it, but Steven, dressed and showered, slid on stocking feet into the kitchen to grab it.

She stood uncertainly by the bed. Esther began talking in undertones to Mei, and she didn't want to overhear. The doorbell rang, and she narrowly missed the doorjamb in her haste to leave the room.

Mrs. Harmel stood waiting on the front steps. Opening the door, Miriam was hit with the unmistakable smell of warm yeast overlaid by melted sugar. Cinnamon rolls. The smell of house calls and murmured commiseration. This morning Mrs. Harmel was fully dressed, and her feet were protected in heavy winter boots. The old woman pressed the warm pan into Miriam's hands.

"I know you don't feel hungry." Mrs. Harmel smiled kindly. "But you must eat. Keep up your strength."

Steven called from the kitchen. "Miriam, that was your father-in-law, calling from the plane. They'll be arriving at ten."

Ben thundered down the stairs and peered over Miriam's shoulder, kissing her on the cheek from behind. "Cinnamon rolls," he exclaimed.

Mrs. Harmel laughed, clearly pleased. "You can have two, young man," she said.

Miriam handed the pan to Ben, who took them into the kitchen. "You want to have a roll and cup of coffee with us, Mrs. Harmel?"

"No need. I have a piece of toast in the morning with my multivitamin and blood pressure pills. Before I go, I just need to know how many will be here tonight."

"How many?" Miriam shook her head, confused.

"Family and friends will come over tonight, I imagine. How many do you think?"

"I'm not sure."

"Never mind. I'll plan for ten." Then, noticing the look on Miriam's face, clarified, "I'll bring dinner over tonight so you don't have to worry about anything." She squeezed Miriam's hand and held it tight for a moment before turning to leave.

Miriam's stomach churned, and she had just enough time to make it into the master bathroom. She remained kneeling for longer than necessary, watching the water in the toilet swirl and disappear.

She pushed herself off the floor and got ready to shower, but couldn't bring herself to step into The Love Cave—the shower stall with dual heads and earth-toned tiles—which they discovered the day they moved in was not actually conducive to love. Water is a lousy lubricant and the walls grated like sandpaper against their backs. "Ready to exfoliate?" Paul liked to say in a husky voice, pressing himself against her whenever they showered together.

A bath would be better. The tub was dusty from disuse, so Miriam rinsed it out, wondering if she had any bubble bath. In the cabinet below the bathroom sink, her fingers unearthed objects long forgotten. An unopened battery-operated foot massager Theresa had given them several

Christmases before. She tossed it in the trash-can. Something shone yellow in the shadows of the cabinet. A pad of sticky notes, the back missing so dust and hair stuck to the adhesive. Into the trash. And there was her favorite pen and a pair of scissors that had been missing for months. When she had asked Paul where these things were, he had gotten mad, saying she had no right to accuse without evidence. Sometimes being married to a lawyer was irritating.

No matter. She didn't want them anymore. She dumped handfuls of objects into the trash, not bothering to look at them. It was satisfying to see order cutting through the disorder, to sweep up the dust and leave the cabinet empty. She opened a drawer, saw the pregnancy kit Paul had brought home a month before, banged it shut, and moved on.

This had been her role when her mother died: cleaning, organizing, throwing away. Her mother had had a stroke early one morning after Miriam left for work, and before she died, had had just enough strength to call Theresa. That was one of the painful mysteries of her life. Why, with her last breath, had she called Theresa? By the time Miriam got home that evening, Theresa had taken care of "the body" and all the funeral arrangements, never seeming to think that she should have called Miriam immediately to come home. By default, Miriam dealt with the house and her mother's belongings alone. She took trip after trip to the church, where they were always looking for food to serve at functions, her car filled with Mason jars of homemade stew, raspberry jam, green beans, some vacuum-sealed, some stored in the freezer, others with a layer of hardened wax on the top. In every room except her own, she found bags of mealy flour, potatoes sprouting long tendrils, rice, dried beans.

The smell of Mrs. Harmel's cinnamon rolls wafted into the bathroom, and Miriam resisted the urge to gag. Under cotton balls, Miriam found a plastic tube of bath beads. Not the same as bubble bath, but perhaps Mei would like the soft balls that clumped solidly together like a swollen rosary. She scratched at them with her finger, and several came loose, sticking to her skin.

Esther called to her through the door.

"Yes?"

"Steven just left to pick up your in-laws."

"Okay." She hastily plucked the beads from her fingertips, tossing them into the trash. That gave her at least an hour. She twisted her hair into a bun on the top of her head, her need for Paul a flash of lightning in her gut, and crouched in an inch of tepid water, shivering as she scrubbed her skin with a rough washcloth.

Like a plague, word was spreading, causing friends to pause in their Sunday routines to call, ask questions, offer up stunned expressions. Miriam, Esther, and even Ben took turns answering the phone. Someone on Paul's baseball team called to ask what she planned to do with his kayak. Esther told him to go to hell and slammed the receiver down.

At this, Mei, who had been on her stomach in the family room, engrossed with cutting construction paper into long strips and, the adults had thought, not paying any attention to their conversation, popped up onto her knees, an extremely satisfied look on her face. Both Miriam and Ben turned their backs to hide their laughter, and Esther said through clenched teeth, "Shut up, you guys. Don't you dare make me laugh."

When Steven returned with Paul's parents, the house felt three sizes too small. Martha's embrace was soft and unbalanced, as though she would topple over the moment Miriam let go, while Henry stood tall and stiff as a tree, thumping her back when she hugged him. After introductions, the room fell awkwardly silent for having six adults in it. Even Mei was subdued, standing close to her mother. Steven broke the spell by mentioning their appointment at the funeral home. Miriam got her coat, and she, Henry, Martha, and Steven headed back out, leaving Esther and Ben at the house to field phone calls.

In the showroom of the funeral home, over a rush of forced air, fluorescent lights buzzed. Caskets lined the room, each partly open to display fluffs of material and small pillows. Each model gleamed, whether red, metallic, or plain wood. Miriam felt suddenly hot and shrugged off her coat, holding it tightly against her chest.

Martha gripped Miriam's arm. They made eye contact, and Martha's lips twitched upward, not an expression to cheer or even to encourage, but one that took the other in, acknowledging the unique yet connected blow each had received. Her mother-in-law's grip was fierce, belying her unremarkable eyes that rarely seemed to have life in them. She was a large woman, bent under layers of extra flesh, which had also led Miriam to judge her as soft and ineffectual. Miriam felt surprise and shame for not believing all along that Martha possessed reserves of hidden strength.

The funeral director, Mr. Larkin, a tall man whose gangly body and high-pitched voice appeared to be stuck in adolescence, seemed ill at ease. Rather than leaving them to look at the caskets on their own, he talked about each one in nervous detail, pointing to the durability of steel, the timeless beauty of mahogany, the fold-away handles for pallbearers.

Martha moved to a casket the color of honey and ran both hands back and forth along the smooth top.

"You'll also notice that in each casket are displayed the different linings. You can choose the fabric as well as style. Satin, for instance, or linen . . ."

Steven stood close to Miriam, arms crossed over his slightly protruding belly, watchful and listening.

". . . velvet, tucked, shirred, fitted . . ."

Henry interacted with each casket, examining finishes, jiggling handles, pressing one or both hands into the depths of the box as if to test his weight against the comfort of the various cushions, unaware of the way his movements made Mr. Larkin's hands flutter.

"How do people decide?" Miriam asked no one in particular.

"Whatever seems most important to you," answered Mr. Larkin. "Some people like one wood better than another,

others like stainless steel. Some decide based on the color of
their spouse's hair—"

"—Are you kidding me?" she said.

He shrugged as if to say he had nothing to do with it.

"Finances," Steven said. "Money is a factor, too."

Henry looked up from his examination of bronze fixtures.
"Price is not important."

"Actually, it's a serious and valid consideration for
Miriam," Steven contradicted.

"I'll pay for it. Price will not be a factor for my son."

"What?" Miriam was taken aback. "Why would you
pay? I can't let you do that."

"No arguments." He glared at her, then turned back to
examine a little treasure drawer, where loved ones could
stash jewelry or ball caps or notes or whatever else they
could think of.

She looked helplessly at Martha, who was no longer
rubbing her hands back and forth, but stood, palms flat
against the coffin lid. Steven merely raised his eyebrows
and shoulders ever so slightly.

"Which one do you like?" Mr. Larkin asked.

"None of them."

His hands rose like sparrows, alighting on the knot in his
tie.

Steven put his arm around her shoulders.

"Here," Henry proclaimed. "This one's good. Solid."
His knuckle thumped the side twice. "But I don't like the
gold hinges and designs. Silver would be better." The lid
had a rope-like molding, the sides heavy with gold

appliqué. The wood was dark walnut, the color of their kitchen cabinets. Miriam's mouth opened in shock once again.

"This is the one." Martha's voice, unheard until this moment, was barely more than a murmur, but every head swiveled as if she had used a megaphone.

"This is the one," she repeated, her hands once again caressing the plain, honey-colored casket. "And Henry will pay for it." Her voice assumed such authority that even he didn't protest.

"Okay," he said, hooking his thumbs into his belt loops and going back on his heels. He nodded in Mr. Larkin's direction. "That one. And I'll pay."

It didn't take long for Mr. Larkin to gather the rest of the information he needed. Behind him, a window revealed an expanse of dull clouds, yet his mahogany desk, lacquered like a coffin, managed to capture enough light to glint painfully against Miriam's eyes. She was glad to finally thank him and shake his hand, but when she stood to go, Henry leaned back in his chair, extending his legs and blocking the doorway.

"Now let's talk about the funeral," he said.

"Yeah, we'll do that now. We've got an appointment with Father Jake—"

"How about you sit down and we deal with it here. There's a nice room here that I'm sure Ted—can I call you Ted?—would let us use for the funeral." He turned to the director, who paled. "Isn't that right?"

Again, Miriam looked to Martha for help, but she was sitting with eyes focused on the floor, not listening, or simply incapable of taking part. Had her mother-in-law's earlier decree been a fluke? Miriam swayed slightly and touched the edge of Mr. Larkin's desk for balance. Had Henry really said this was costing him too much to not have a say in where the funeral was held? Surely not. She dropped back into her chair.

"Paul wanted a Catholic funeral," Steven said.

"What do you know about it?" Henry demanded.

"He and Miriam talked about it. Specifically."

Miriam nodded. "We did. We both wanted our funerals at Immaculate Heart."

"I didn't raise my son to be a holy roller. Now that he's dead," he paused for effect, "it's time for you to show me and my family some respect."

Martha closed her eyes and dropped her chin to her chest.

"Just because you don't share the same faith as your son doesn't mean you have the right to say that," Steven said, standing, as if ready for a fight.

Miriam had never heard this tone of voice from Steven. Her father-in-law's face had gone white, his thin mouth a slice of red above a thick chin. He shifted to get out of his seat, and Miriam popped out of her chair. "You know what? I don't think Paul would want us to fight over this. Let's just have the funeral here. I think that would probably be best." She reached for Steven's hand and pushed at him, gently, until he sat down. "Would that be okay, Mr. Larkin? Do you have a room we could use?"

The arrangements made, Miriam left the funeral home, followed by Henry, Martha, and Steven.

"I have an appointment to keep with Father Jake," she told Henry. "Would you like me to drop you off at the house first?"

"You better not get that priest involved," he declared.

In the church office, Miriam and Steven were told that Father Jake was with another parishioner, but would be out in a few minutes. Miriam fled the secretary's pitiful gaze and entered the shadows of the sanctuary, the door closing behind them with a sigh. Steven settled onto a pew, but she remained standing. She could tell he was unhappy with the way she had given in to Henry.

"Miriam, can I ask you a question?"

She turned to face the wall, placing both hands flat against the cool stones, pressing her fingertips into the rough surface. At eye level was a cubby where a saint perched, stone toes peeking out from under his robe. Waiting for Steven's question, which she was sure she didn't want to hear, much less answer, she counted the toes.

"I was just wondering—"

"Did Mom ever teach you this prayer?" she interrupted him. "I place my Catholic soul before Thee, and in my despair and anguish, beseech Thee to bring the most powerful strength of Thy Helping Hand to come to my rescue. I place the devotion of my sorrowful heart at Thy feet that I may be pardoned from a destiny of suffering." Three toes showed beneath the fold in the saint's robe. She had a hard time believing saints had things like toes. Digits were too human. Too average.

She turned to look at Steven. "No?" she said, when he didn't answer her. "That was the prayer Mom taught me after Vinny died. When I got home from the hospital, we prayed it every day. Without fail." She walked to the next cubby, where the saint had no toes showing. "I wonder why she taught me that prayer at that particular time. Doesn't it seem, oh, I don't know. Obsolete? Since Edward and Vinny were already dead?" She turned and leaned against the wall, waiting for Steven to respond.

He had his head in his hands and finally spoke through his fingers. "Maybe the better question is: What kind of sick, twisted woman would teach her nine-year-old such a prayer?"

"Here you are." Father Jake's voice startled them both. "I'm glad you're here," he said, shaking Steven's hand somberly and then turning to engulf Miriam in an embrace.

With her head pressed against his shoulder, she heard him say, "Oh," several times, quietly, as if anything else would be too much. Although he was quite a bit shorter than her brother, he had always reminded her of Steven. The same round body and spiky gray hair; the same breathtaking hugs; the same eyes that penetrated deep into her core. Miriam surprised herself by feeling as though she might finally cry. But the impulse receded when he released her.

Before they left the sanctuary, Miriam turned to Steven. "Please don't be mad at me," she pleaded. He squeezed her shoulder, and she leaned against him on the way to Father Jake's office.

# five

When Theresa looked Miriam up and down with her lips pursed in disapproval, Miriam thought with a sinking feeling, *So this is how today's going to go.*

"Bad idea?" she asked, plucking at one of the fuzzy yellow sleeves of the Tango sweater, which she had chosen in lieu of a black blazer, feeling the rightness of this decision as the soft shag caressed her arms.

"Not if you're starring in a parade."

Shame flushed Miriam's cheeks. She left the sweater with her coat, regretting now the sleeveless dress. She rubbed her chilly arms, waiting for Mr. Larkin to finish directing the stragglers to the few remaining seats so they could get started. Peeking around the doorway, Miriam was amazed by how crowded the room was. She felt tired to think she'd have to sustain conversations with each one over the course of the day.

As she moved down the narrow aisle with Steven beside her and the rest of the family following, silence spread outward like the waves from a stone dropped in a pond. She was aware of the suspended sentences, the heads turning her way, the eyes trying to gauge how the young widow was doing.

Charles stepped to the podium, faltering over his first few words, but gaining control. He talked awhile, followed first by Henry and then Paul's boss, Todd Jennings, and then he invited others to share as well. Henry had been pleased with this idea, of turning the funeral into little more than a memorial service where people could tell humorous or touching anecdotes about Paul. In another setting, Miriam would covet every story, over a cold beer, perhaps, in a dark restaurant or on someone's back porch after the sun had gone down, but here? It felt sacrilegious. The talk should be of Paul's soul, not the funny thing he did in the fourth grade.

Henry was sitting forward in his seat, hyper-alert, eyes glued to whoever was bending earnestly into the microphone. Martha was weeping into a wad of tissue, but her tears appeared to be laced with gratefulness over the evidence of how much people loved and would miss her son.

Miriam had trouble concentrating. She drew her tongue across her front teeth to check for lipstick, then felt appalled for caring about such things. She fingered her necklace, a tarnished silver chain that held a medallion of Saint

Genevieve that she had worn since she was confirmed at age thirteen.

Earlier that morning, as Esther used a thousand pins to hold Miriam's hair in a French twist, they had talked about how many funerals they had been to. Esther's grandfather had died when she was a child, but most of her relatives were either healthy or still living and dying in China. She had never even been to the funeral of an acquaintance. This was Miriam's fourth, counting both her parents and Steven's lover who had died of cancer when she was in high school. She hadn't been present at either of her brothers' funerals, though they were so much a part of her consciousness that sometimes she thought she must've been. Miriam couldn't fathom life without the occasional burial and trips to the cemetery every Memorial Day to tend the graves.

When her father was buried, Miriam was only twenty-five, and she squeezed out a few tears, not because she would miss him, although she would in theory, but because she had already learned that's what one does at funerals. Her tears ceased, however, the moment she saw Steven crying silently, both hands covering his face, his fingers pushing his glasses onto his forehead. Loneliness pierced her, watching him struggle to contain himself, because she couldn't comprehend—hadn't anticipated—his grief. Despite their closeness, she might as well have been in a different country, so little did she understand what was taking place within him. She thought to go to him, but feared his rejection in case he didn't want her near. She never did ask what their father's death meant to him, why it had hit him so hard, afraid she might not be strong enough to handle her older brother's pain. Now she slipped her arm under Steven's and held tightly to his hand. He shifted, and returned the pressure.

Before she knew it, Charles was welcoming everyone to join them at the cemetery before heading to Theresa and Carl's home for the luncheon.

Following right behind the hearse, they took slow turns on the winding road of the cemetery, and Miriam watched the rows of gravestones go by, struck by how unfamiliar they looked. She hadn't realized how much she had come to know her family's cemetery, not only their actual graves, but the names and shapes of the markers of all the others buried there, too. She wondered again at her decision to do as Henry wished and exclude Father from the service, which meant burying Paul here among all these strangers rather than with the rest of her family in the Catholic cemetery.

When she stepped out of the car, she looked down the long procession of cars, each with a flag on its roof, snaking all the way back to the entrance and onto the main road. People began making their way slowly toward her, the sound of their car doors a soft staccato in the chill air.

Mr. Larkin helped the pallbearers move the casket into place, and one of his assistants directed Miriam to one of three canvas chairs where he draped a blanket over her knees. It was a dark avocado color, coarse and heavy. Martha squeezed into the chair next to her, and Theresa took the last one. The men would stand behind.

Despite the biting wind, people gathered in loose clusters wherever snow had been adequately cleared rather than pressing close together for warmth. Miriam craned her neck. She spotted Esther staring into space, cradling Mei in her arms and swaying back and forth. The little girl was sucking her thumb, cheek pressed against her mother's shoulder. There was one of Paul's childhood friends. A few of her co-workers. Lawyers. As Miriam's glance traveled past groups of people, she caught numerous eyes shifting away from hers. Near the hearse, there was a glimpse of white, and her pulse quickened, thinking it was Father Jake in one of his ornately embroidered robes and terrified Henry would see him, although this was precisely what she had been searching—hoping—for.

Charles took charge again, and while he read Scripture— "dust to dust"—and said a brief prayer, which was apparently acceptable to Henry, who reverently bowed his head, it didn't carry the weight or comforting authority as it would have if Father had been the one using the exact same words.

To strengthen her resolve, Miriam tried to imagine what would have happened if she had defied Henry in this. Although her father-in-law was generally on his best behavior around her, she sensed a latent fire beneath the surface, a hard core of anger, a cruelty she could not fathom.

Once before, at her wedding, she had turned to meet her father-in-law's gaze and witnessed firsthand his true feelings. In the reflection of his chiseled jaw, the calculating glint of his eyes, she saw herself as something to be wiped

off the bottom of his shoe. It wasn't just that he disagreed
with her faith. It was personal.

*Yes*, she thought, with hard-earned fortitude, as she listened to Charles's simple prayer over Paul's grave. *It's better
this way.*

When the casket was lowered, Miriam stood to drop the
first handful of cold dirt on top. This was one of the only
things she had insisted on. Her family had always witnessed
the lowering of the casket, and she could not be swayed,
even by Mr. Larkin, who felt the newer tradition of walking
away before that happened was for the best.

She had expected the dirt to be frozen hard, but it felt
strangely warm and damp, just this side of mud. She looked
at her hand in surprise, and before she knew what she was
doing, brushed a finger across her right cheek. Theresa,
after dropping a rose and crossing herself, dug a tissue out
of her purse and handed it to Miriam, who looked at it
blankly. Theresa took it back and used it to wipe Miriam's
face. Miriam closed her eyes at the unexpected tenderness
with which Theresa touched her.

"At least you didn't have any children," said Jenny, the
wife of photography-enthusiast Kevin. She and Jenny often
sat next to each other during their husbands' baseball
games, lamenting having to share their spouses with the
sport.

Miriam had just stepped into the cavernous foyer of
Theresa's house and was having trouble prying her eyes

away from the Christmas garland and twinkling white lights that wound up the banister to the second floor. She had managed to forget what time of year it was, other than winter.

Ben stood sentry, gathering coats in his arms and taking the stairs two at a time to deposit them in an upstairs bedroom. Esther was pulled away by Mei, who was doing an awkward bird dance down the hallway, thighs pressed together, in dire need of a bathroom. A lot of people had arrived already.

"I mean," Jenny continued, "it would be awful to have to explain death to a little kid."

"Thank God for small blessings, right?" Miriam answered, hating herself for the sarcasm, though she could usually count on Jenny to miss it.

"Exactly." This was one of Jenny's favorite expressions. Egg-ZAK-lee: useful for emphasis, agreement, or whenever there was space in a conversation that needed to be filled. "Hey. I met Paul's parents last night at the wake. They're not what I expected. Paul doesn't look like either of them, does he?"

"No, he doesn't."

Jenny's face fell. "Oh," she said, her eyes brimming.

"It's okay," Miriam whispered to her friend, meaning that it was okay to cry, okay to use the wrong tense, okay to say whatever came to mind.

"No, it's not," Jenny replied, crying in earnest. "Nothing's okay."

Miriam handed her a tissue, and together they moved into the central living room where the gas fireplace was blazing.

Standing close to it, but still cold, Miriam thought with regret of her sweater, which was lying in the car.

For a long time, Miriam was able to stay near the fire and allow people to come to her. She smiled a lot, an effortful manipulation of the lips and cheek muscles, said thank you a million times, and doled out hugs as often as tissue. There was comfort in knowing that each person there cared about her, cared about Paul.

Bob Carley loomed large, his personality bursting against the seams of his dark suit, his magnetism out of place.

"Don't worry about me," he said as soon as he saw her, when in truth, she hadn't given him or her duties at work a single thought during the week she had missed so far. "Take all the time you need." He planted his hands heavily on her shoulders and spoke slowly, as if she didn't speak English well.

She looked up at him in surprise, because as she squeaked out a feeble "thank you," she realized that she had no intention of going back to work. She patted his arm tenderly and said, "I appreciate that. Really."

When he headed toward a small group of her other co-workers, Miriam slipped into the hallway. In the next room the small, one-person canoe Paul had been crafting by hand leaned upright in a corner. A man touched his fingertip to a rough place where Paul's sandpaper hadn't had time to reach, making her feel strangely violated. She thought he might be the one who had asked for Paul's kayak.

Miriam heard a woman's voice drifting down the staircase and thought at first it was Martha. But it was Mrs. Harmel, who had been upstairs to get her coat. She made her way down slowly, taking one step at a time, clinging tightly to the banister with both hands.

"I could've gotten your coat for you!" Miriam called to her.

"No, honey, I'm fine. Slow, but fine."

When the old woman reached the bottom step, Miriam took her elbow, feeling how thin she was underneath the winter jacket. "Do you need a ride home, Mrs. Harmel?"

"Heavens, no. A friend is coming to pick me up. She and I go out to lunch once a week, so I asked her to pick me up here. Ben," she leaned close to Miriam's ear and whispered confidentially, "who is such a handsome young man, called her a little while ago with directions."

"Well, I appreciate your being here. And thanks for all the food you've brought over."

"She's a widow, too, you know."

"Who?" Miriam asked, confused. "Who's a widow?"

"Her husband, rest his soul, wouldn't let her drive, so the week after he passed, she signed up for lessons. Has been driving for fifteen years now."

The doorbell rang, and Miriam opened it to a woman who looked older than her neighbor.

"There you are!" yelled Mrs. Harmel, startling Miriam. In a normal tone of voice: "She's deaf as a post."

The old ladies linked arms and made their way down the driveway with tiny steps. Mrs. Harmel's friend slipped a little, and Miriam gasped, watching until they were both safely in the car. It was a wonder the woman could see over the steering wheel.

When Miriam turned from the door, a woman she didn't know was waiting for her. "You are Mrs. Kovatch," the woman said in a heavily accented voice. Her brown hair, streaked with thick patches of gray, was pulled back in a jumbled ponytail that would tangle painfully when she took out the elastic band.

Miriam nodded.

"I want to ask how are you, but is stupid question." She looked away nervously, stepping aside as someone needed to get past them.

"Don't worry. I know what you mean." Miriam tried to imagine how this woman knew Paul. Her accent, her bright clothes—an orange, flowered blouse with powder blue pants—and her glittery blue eye shadow gave her the look of someone from a depressed country, of someone reveling in the astounding choices of a Western economy. Yet in her eyes was a confident kindness that attracted Miriam.

"My name is Svetlana," and then she said a last name that included a "xha" sound from the back of her throat that Miriam could not have repeated if her life depended on it. "I know your husband. He helped me incredibly much." All her h's were pronounced "xha." Another person squeezed past them, and this seemed to disconcert Svetlana.

"Let's go in there," Miriam said, leading her toward the front of the house to a smaller room where there were fewer people. She sat on the love seat and motioned Svetlana next to her. They sat slightly crooked, facing each other, outer knees touching. Miriam watched Svetlana gather her thoughts. She couldn't tell if it was the language barrier that was giving her trouble, or what she wanted to say.

Svetlana seemed to come to a decision. "I have been married twenty-five years," she stated. "My husband and I come here two years ago, and he thought maybe life would not be so hard. He drank very much and he was, I think you say, a mean drunk. At first I think I am deserving this treatment, because I am the one who wanted to come to America. But Mr. Kovatch, your husband, tells me this is a lie. I have no money to pay him, but he was helping me with a divorce anyway, and also to find work and most of all, to find safety. It is my husband who should be dead, not yours," she concluded. "I am not ashamed to say this."

Miriam felt powerless to respond.

Svetlana's chin sank into the collar of her blouse, apparently spent.

They sat, in silence strangely companionable, and people passed by them as if they were invisible.

*m*iriam's dreams began to filter into her waking life.

The sound of a strange man's voice, the clang of a door

slamming shut, the panic of having misplaced something important. Stabs of déjà vu came to her at odd times, like an echo from a previous life. She did not normally remember her dreams, and now she wondered if she was perhaps getting too much sleep. Yet most nights, she tossed and wrestled with the sheets, and in the morning, faced each day with a feeling of utter exhaustion.

One night, she relived an ominously altered honeymoon. They were kayaking in the Boundary Waters, and the sky was bright, as it had been in reality, a clear blue that was reflected brilliantly in the lake. The sun beat pleasantly against her bare shoulders, something she knew would make her freckles more pronounced and lighten the hair on her arms. She paused briefly between strokes, holding the paddle perpendicular to the kayak, watching water trail off it, marring the smooth surface of the water. Along the densely forested shoreline, a dark shadow between two evergreens took on the shape of a moose with strips of loosened fur dangling from an enormous rack on its head. She wondered at the animal's power as it languidly lowered its muzzle to the ground and raised its head again, watchful, jaws working, as if the antlers were no heavier than foam. A loon called, its voice riding the waves, and Miriam turned toward the sound, her paddle accidentally slapping the water.

Paul's kayak nosed into view next to her, but she shushed him, commanding, "Listen," knowing instantly it was a mistake, for when she looked, he was gone. There, at the edge of a far island, was his empty kayak. The paddle blistered her palms, and she felt the shaky tiredness of her muscles as she pulled hard against the water. Once on shore, she ran down an overgrown path, long grass and brambles whipping her calves, catching brief glimpses of Paul's green windbreaker. Unable to run any longer, doubled over and lungs aching, she called his name, hearing in reply the thunderous crashes of the moose running away, the sharp cry of squirrels warning each other of her presence.

She surfaced from the dream in her tangled bed with the feeling that she had been trying to scream, that her strangled noises had woken her. Figment, who had taken to sleeping on her pillow, was lying on her hair. She tossed him to the foot of the bed, where he protested with a long meow before flopping heavily against her legs.

She stared at the glowing numbers of the alarm clock, waiting for her heart to slow.

Paul had taken fishing trips to the Boundary Waters in northern Minnesota several times before he met her, and had loved it so much that when he suggested they go there for their honeymoon, she hadn't had the heart to show him the travel books of Italy she had been poring over. Once in the Boundary Waters, she had understood the appeal: a chain of impossibly clear lakes dotted with small islands where no motorboats were allowed and it was possible to catch enough fish to eat well every evening. They kayaked and portaged through the tiniest sliver of the million-acre wilderness with only the most basic supplies, camping on a different island every night for ten days and glimpsing only two other people in the far distance. The solitude and proximity of wildlife felt to her like a disparate, dreamed-of world. The experience brought into sharp focus how steeped she was in the overwrought noise of "civilized life."

She had loved the loons especially, how they would lounge on the water and then disappear suddenly, only to pop up hundreds of feet away with a fish dangling from their beak. The birds' ominous cries at night, undulating across the black, thrilled her. She tried to imagine what it would be like to hear the sound for the first time without any knowledge of what made it; wondered if the sound had spawned legends of unhappy spirits roaming the wilderness and crying out their misery.

She got up for a drink of water before trying to fall back to sleep. Nightmare or not, she didn't want to dream of the honeymoon again.

Although Miriam never did decorate or put up a tree, Christmas came, and along with it, the usual array of social obligations. Sympathy apparently motivated people to send cards, as the unusually tall pile on the dining room table could attest. After the first ten or eleven, she stopped opening them.

Charles and Esther stayed with her for a few days past the funeral, and although her pulse accelerated painfully at unpredictable times—in the shower; at three in the morning; when the mailman snapped shut the lid of the mailbox—she was relieved to see her company go. She was tired. Tired of avoiding her bedroom, of making small talk, of eating three times a day and pretending she wasn't having trouble keeping everything down.

On the way to Theresa's for their traditional Christmas Eve dinner of spaghetti, Miriam's car sputtered and gasped. She frantically examined the dashboard, noting the blinking low-fuel light. The car struggled forward, and as she inched through a green light, praying to make it past the intersection, she saw a gas station less than a block away. Rolling to a stop next to the pump, she crossed herself, murmuring a quick word of thanks to St. Nicholas.

Stepping out of the car, Miriam felt cold air crackling inside her nostrils. She slipped her credit card into the pump, hurrying against the wind, annoyed when she realized she had forgotten to release the cover of the gas tank. She grappled for the lever by the front seat, popped the cover and tried to twist open the underlying cap. It wouldn't budge. She tried again. Nothing. Anger flared, hot in her chest. She took her gloves off with her teeth and twisted as hard as she could on the cap. It opened with a jerk, catching her thumb against the hinge of the cover. The metal took a gouge out of her knuckle, and she watched the pores slowly turn red as blood rose to the surface.

The little latch that would allow the gas to pump automatically so she could wait in the warm car until the tank filled was disabled, and Miriam's anger grew, turning toward herself.

Her thanks to St. Nicholas had been reflexive, she realized, given her years of parochial schooling and her devout mother. Miriam used to think nothing was too trivial for God's attention. The smallest flicker of pain, the tiniest inconvenience, the most inconsequential decision could be held up for God's consideration. But juxtaposed against Paul's death, she couldn't help feeling the apparent trivialness of this belief. To think that Nicholas would perform a miracle when she ran out of gas so she didn't have to walk half a block while the patron saint of lawyers, St. Thomas More, not to mention God himself, had looked the other way while her husband was gasping on the sidewalk. . . .

Better not finish that thought. Without waiting for the receipt to print, Miriam pulled away from the station, knuckles white on the steering wheel.

When she arrived at Theresa's, she was shocked to see Steven's truck already there. He and Theresa had not spoken in years, so the only time he had been involved in family Christmases was when Miriam hosted. And then the two of them would carefully avoid each other, filling the air with muted tension. She tried, and failed, to imagine Theresa calling Steven to invite him over.

Ben ran outside without a coat to greet her.

"Are you crazy? You're going to catch pneumonia!"

"Give me those." He held out his arms to take the presents from her.

At the threshold, Ben hesitated. His amber eyes reflected glints of color from the Christmas lights that climbed the pillars on either side of the door. His breath billowed white in front of his face before the wind took it away.

"What is it?" Miriam asked, managing to squash her impulse to ask if they could talk inside.

"I already got Uncle Paul's present."

The wind worked its way under Miriam's coat and bit at her legs. She waited.

"I got him two season tickets to my football games next year."

"That's a wonderful gift. He would've loved to see you play."

"I can't take them back." He looked at her expectantly.

"Could you sell them?" She could tell by his face this was the wrong thing to say.

"I thought maybe you'd like them."

She shifted her weight from one foot to the other.

"It's a pair of tickets and Dad could come with you. He's talked about seeing more of my games since it'll be my senior year."

"Maybe your mom should have the extra ticket so she and your dad can go together." The wrongness of this, too, made her flinch. Before she could back track, Ben was inside, disappearing down the hall.

Carl met her in the foyer, and, after helping her out of her coat, pulled her into a big hug. She could count on two hands the times he had hugged her, but she lingered in his arms, her cheek pressed against his hard chest, fiercely soaking up his embrace. He patted her on the back several times, then, with his arm around her shoulders, walked her to the living room. "We're just waiting for Theresa to call us to dinner," he explained.

"I'll go help her."

"No, come sit with us. Theresa is . . . how shall I put it?" He paused and then lowered his voice. "She's in a bit of a snit."

"Is that what you call it?" Ben said sarcastically, from the floor by the tree, where he was adding Miriam's presents to the pile.

"It's either that or something I would be condemned for saying in front of my offspring."

Steven was sitting in an armchair next to the fire. She leaned down to kiss him, then curled up in the corner of the couch nearest him.

"Rum and coke for you, Miriam?" Carl asked.

"Better not. It might put me to sleep."

"Ah, never mind that. You can stay here and get up with Theresa at the crack of dawn to dress the turkey."

"My dream come true."

"How about some eggnog?"

She made a face.

"Not out of a carton. Homemade." Carl wiggled his fingers in the air like a surgeon who has just scrubbed. "Come on, you've got to try some."

The sight of the thick, yellowish cream gave her pause, but when she cautiously sniffed the glass he handed her, it smelled richly soothing. She sipped. Foam trailed warmly down her throat.

He looked pleased. "Didn't know I had it in me, did you?"

"If I'd known it was your concoction, I would've turned you down," Steven said, holding up his empty glass for a refill.

"Ben, why don't you get your trebuchet to show Steven and Miriam," Carl suggested, taking a seat at the other end of the couch.

Ben shrugged moodily.

"What's a trebuchet?" Steven asked.

"First, could you spell it for me?" Miriam said.

"Tre-boo-shay," Ben pronounced. "Hang on. I'll get it."

While he was out of the room, Theresa came in to announce that dinner was ready. She did look annoyed at something.

"Ben's gone to get his trebuchet," Carl told her.

Miriam expected Theresa to say that Ben could wait, but instead she said, "Would you get me some of that?" indicating the eggnog, and when he had given her a glass, she settled on the couch next to Carl, pulling her feet under her. Steven gave Miriam a look of surprise.

There was a clatter in the hallway, and Ben wheeled a three-foot-high wooden catapult into the room. Once he had it positioned in front of the fireplace, he got on his knees to explain its intricacies.

"See, you put whatever you want to throw, like a cannon-ball, over here and a bunch of rocks or sand on the other side to use as a counterweight. Then you use this rope to winch the cannonball down," he turned a crank that slowly pulled one side of the trebuchet down. "A pin goes in the chain right here to hold it."

"Let's see you toss something," Steven said.

"How about a potato," Carl suggested. "Aim for the top of the tree."

"Yeah, right," Theresa said, smacking him.

"What?" he said, innocently. "It's coming down soon anyway."

Theresa giggled.

"Didn't you make some fruitcake this year, Theresa?" Steven goaded. "That could do some damage."

"I happen to know you like fruitcake, buster," she retorted. "Keep talking and just see if you get any."

Miriam, bemused by their banter, turned her attention back to the catapult. "Where on earth did you get this thing?"

"I made it," Ben said, with apparent nonchalance. "I've been working with my history professor on it all year. It's an exact replica of a trebuchet detailed in an old manuscript he discovered."

"This was what they actually used?"

"Yeah. To attack the walls around castles and cities in medieval times. Professor Lynch is going to Scotland with a bunch of other scientists for three weeks this summer to build a full-size version."

"Wish I had a job like that," Steven said.

"And? What else?" Theresa prompted Ben.

"And he's invited me to go with him."

Ben, embarrassed by Steven and Miriam's exclamations, busied himself with releasing the tension on the chain. Theresa and Carl had enormous smiles on their faces. Miriam noted their expressions and blinked back tears of relief for Ben, that although she didn't see it often, his parents were proud of him.

"Come on, let's eat." Theresa stood, breaking the spell.

Over dinner, Theresa spoke to Ben impatiently when he was slow to hear someone talking to him, even if it was just to request the salad or spaghetti. He seemed absorbed and distant, euphoria over the trebuchet and his trip to Scotland quickly gone. Miriam avoided the spicy sauce on her plate, ate bits of warm garlic bread.

Steven was seated next to her, and she was grateful for his presence and for the fact that the seat next to her was not empty. Along with Ben, she had difficulty adding to the conversation.

"Carl," Theresa said, "I doubt anyone here is interested in how technology stocks are doing at this time of year."

Undaunted, Carl said, "Nonsense. It's what keeps this country afloat. Not the government, not Bill Gates. The stock market." He pointed his fork at Theresa. "And anyway, I saw you checking your stocks on-line this morning. You can pretend you were surfing for recipes, but I know the Nasdaq when I see it."

Theresa's cheeks reddened. "Hmph," she said.

Ben abruptly left the table. Theresa started to call him back, but Carl placed his hand on hers. "Let him go," he said. Everyone stared down at their plates for a while before Carl roused himself to ask Steven how the upholstery business was going.

Miriam excused herself and crept upstairs, where she found Ben on his bed, an arm flung over his eyes. She sat next to him and placed her hand on his chest, feeling the movement of his rib cage as he breathed. He didn't move at her touch.

"I don't know how everyone can act like nothing happened," he said.

"I think everyone's just trying to hold it together."

Ben uncovered his eyes to peer at her. "By pretending that it's not completely messed up that Paul's gone?"

She clasped her hands in her lap, miserably, unable to think of anything to say.

"How are you holding it together?" he asked.

"What do you mean?"

"Do you cry all the time at home, when no one's around? Like it would be bad to show emotion with family?"

"No, I—"

"My mom doesn't show emotion," he said bitterly, getting up from the bed and facing the dark window. "God forbid." Suddenly he went into a boxer's stance and punched at the glass, missing by only a hair.

Miriam could tell it took every ounce of his self-control to not crash his fist through the window. She was so stunned that she didn't do anything for a moment before leaping to her nephew and holding him tight. He sobbed on her shoulder, his fingers digging painfully into her back, the muscles of his shoulders remaining tight and hard no matter how long she rubbed them.

She got home late. Figment was so happy to see her he wouldn't leave her side, tangling constantly with her feet. She sat in the hallway next to his food dish, watching him gulp his dinner before turning off the lights and slowly making her way up to the bedroom.

Everything on the dresser was slightly out of order. On Paul's side of the bureau was the square, metal safe where he had kept his cologne, of all things. The safe had been a gag gift from Charles while they were in school and this was how he used it. He would never tell her what cologne he wore or how he'd acquired the bottles—old girlfriends, she guessed—and seemed to get a kick out of hiding something so ridiculous under lock and key. She loved to spring into the bedroom when they were getting ready to go out, catching him with the safe open just to watch him scramble to get everything back inside. "You are the most bizarre human being," she told him. "Certifiable."

That he hid his cologne no longer seemed funny or quirky. What else had he kept from her? She felt hatred for this inanimate object. She turned the dial a few times, knowing she'd never stumble on the combination. He was not the type to write such things down, either. She found a nail file and wedged it into the door, working it up and down. It looked so easy to pick locks in the movies. She yanked at it fiercely, and the safe fell off the dresser with a terrible clank of glass. The smell of cologne rose like a dense fog, nearly causing her to stagger backward. She snatched it up, holding it at arm's length. Liquid dripped from the corner, and she cupped her hand underneath, springing for the garbage. Once it was in a plastic bag, she took it to the garage where she buried it beneath other trash bags, trying to dry her hand on old newspaper.

She made the mistake of smelling her hand and gagged. "This is getting ridiculous," she told Figment as she chased him back into the house.

Even after she scrubbed, the scent clung like a bad memory, enough to make her stomach heave if she wasn't vigilant, and she knew it would be days before it dissipated from the room, the garage, her skin.

Her nausea was starting to take on a life of its own. She couldn't deny it any longer. Reluctantly, she opened the drawer in the bathroom cabinet where Paul had stashed the pregnancy test. He had been so proud of himself for buying it, as if it were a box of condoms and he was fourteen. She picked it up and glanced at the label: 99% accurate. Used in hospitals. Safe and easy.

Might as well get this over with. She unwrapped the plastic wand, uncapped the absorbent cotton and peed on it, as instructed. Recapped it and set it on the back of the toilet. She expected to have a few minutes to wait—a grace period—before it told her anything. But by the time she had flushed the toilet, a first and second line had appeared with a vengeance, one to tell her the test had worked, the other to tell her what she was suddenly petrified to know, thick strokes of blue that floated before her eyes.

She stuffed the wand back into the box and stomped to the garage, where she threw the pregnancy test into the cologne-drenched trash-can. Back upstairs, she grabbed a large trash bag from the hall closet and went into the bedroom, where she yanked open one of Paul's drawers. She dug out handfuls of socks, cramming them into the bag. The underwear drawer emptied quickly. No one would want used underclothes. This she could do. She was good at getting rid of things after people died, good at cleaning up messes.

She ripped open the closet, tearing shirts and suit coats off their hangers with both hands, no longer taking the time to stuff them into the already-full trash bag, just tossing them over her shoulder. The hangers rocked up and down, askew and jangling. She kicked the clothes into the hallway and onto the stairs. Figment dove and pounced, thinking this was a great game. She was trampling a pair of beige pants when she accidentally stepped on Figment's tail. He screeched. She froze as he recovered to burrow in the pile, a paw or nose periodically emerging from the folds.

Then he was on top, scratching at a shirt with his back claws, ripping the fabric.

"Stop that!" she yelled, and, kneeling amidst the disarray, she began to cry.

## seven

*J*anuary was a dreary month. Up and down the block, people put away their Christmas decorations, leaving solitary porch lights to illuminate the otherwise dark houses. Tinsel tangled in the branches of dead trees that lay on the curbs in a spray of pine needles, waiting for the garbage men to come by.

The steering wheel radiated cold into Miriam's hands through her gloves. Snow from the December storms lingered on the ground, old and crusty, blackened by car exhaust. She drove without thought, and when she pulled into a parking space in front of Paul's law office and turned off the ignition, she felt a jolt: She couldn't remember anything about the thirty-minute drive, whether she'd signaled at corners or stopped for red lights. She gave herself a mental shake.

Ginny, the young receptionist, greeted her with an embarrassed look. Usually Miriam breezed past the front door with no more than a wave, but this time Ginny stopped her. "Miriam," she said, the phone already perched on her shoulder. "I'll let Mr. Jennings know you're here."

"That's okay," Miriam said, misunderstanding. "I know my way."

"Still, why don't you have a seat over there, while I call him." Ginny indicated the leather couch. "Can I get you anything? Coffee, water, soda?"

Miriam shook her head and pretended to be absorbed by the artwork on the wall opposite Ginny's desk. It was a six-by-three-foot piece of black and twisted metal soldered to a steel plate. It looked as if a freight train had run over it several times and gave off the faint smell of an old penny that's been lying in the backyard for a few summers. A little plaque beside the sculpture read, "Leviathan Purged."

The first time Miriam saw it, she whispered to Paul, "I don't get it."

"That's because there's nothing to get," he retorted, and then added dryly, "It probably earned someone a Ph.D."

They didn't always agree on decorating. One of their first fights as a married couple was over the larger-than-life poster of Jackie Robinson he wanted to hang in the living room. But "leviathan" became their code word for tacky—everything from pretentious modern architecture to garage-sale, velvet-covered paintings of Elvis.

"Miriam." Todd Jennings took long strides past Ginny's desk and grasped Miriam's hand in both of his. She was embarrassed by her clammy hands.

"You look great," he said, stupidly. "Come on, I'll walk you back."

They passed two secretary cubicles and the conference room that always looked as if a tornado had recently hit, the long table buried under yellow legal pads and leather-bound books. The conference room where the lawyers met with important clients was on the other end of the hall, all leather and crystal goblets for ice water or scotch, if the client was both really important and male. There was a soft murmur of voices and ringing phones from the various rooms they passed.

In Paul's office, Todd clicked on the lights, and there was a moment of hesitation before they flickered on.

Miriam set down the empty box she had brought but felt reluctant to start sifting through things with Todd watching. On the bookshelf directly behind Paul's desk, positioned so clients sitting in one of the chairs facing him would be able to see it, was a framed photo of her. She picked it up. Dust had accumulated in the crevices of the rough frame that was supposed to resemble tree bark, and she swiped at it with her sleeve.

"I'm glad he never knew," she said.

"Knew what?"

"Oh, man." She gave herself another mental shake. "Did I say that out loud? I've gotten so used to talking to my cat, it's become a bad habit. I should probably stop that."

"Better than talking to the vegetables at the grocery store." Todd sat down opposite the desk, ran his fingers through his hair.

"This is such an awful picture of me." She held it out for him to see. She was standing on a trail in what looked like a rain forest but was really northern Minnesota, balancing Paul's backpack against her hip, using her kayak paddle as a rest for her arm. The top of her own pack loomed above her shoulders, and it didn't take a magnifying glass to see that black flies and mosquitoes had spent time on every inch of exposed skin: cheeks, shoulders, arms, legs.

"I was mortified when Paul brought home an eight-by-ten of this and told me he was taking it to work."

"It's from a camping trip, right?"

"Our honeymoon, actually. In the Boundary Waters."

"Let me guess. That was Paul's brainchild."

She smiled, placing the picture face down in the bottom of the box and leaning back against the bookshelf. "We ate reconstituted potatoes, instant cornbread, and fish for lunch and dinner. Every day. Hot off the fire at night, cold leftovers for lunch. Paul wanted to eat fish for breakfast, too, and was completely baffled when I started sobbing into my coffee at the suggestion."

Todd laughed.

"I never told him I would've preferred a trip to Italy or a week on a hot beach where cabana boys could bring me icy drinks with little umbrellas in them."

"Men are idiots. It's taken years for my wife to train me. Even now I still sometimes make the mistake of thinking hot dogs at a Cubs game would make a great date."

Ginny stuck her head in the door. "Mr. Jennings, your three o'clock interview is here."

"I'll be right out. Offer him a cup of coffee." His face flushed, starting at the base of his neck where his adam's apple bobbed every time he swallowed, and Miriam realized he was interviewing for Paul's replacement.

She sat down in Paul's chair, careful not to lean back so it wouldn't squeak.

"Paul was lucky to have you, Miriam," Todd said, quietly, leaning forward, his hands dangling between his knees. He peered at her intently. "You made him really happy."

She dragged her index finger along the length of the desk, watching dust accumulate against her skin.

Todd stood. At the door, he stopped and plunged his hands in his pockets. "Take your time," he said, jangling keys and change. "Let me know if you need anything, okay?"

She flicked the dust onto the floor and gave him a faltering smile. "Thanks," she said, meaning it.

When he was gone, she took the picture out of the box to look at it again. Her hair was frizzy from an early-morning rain, and she had no makeup on, but she was smiling. She had never told anyone, not even Esther, how she felt about that trip. Truthfully, her honeymoon fantasy had always involved satin sheets, leisurely dinners, snorkeling off exotic islands. She put the picture back in the box. She couldn't regret the honeymoon now. Perhaps it was the one good thing she'd done, to give him that trip, to let him think, when he looked at the abominable picture, that she had been having the time of her life. And she had enjoyed the loons.

The long, central drawer of Paul's desk slid open smoothly. It contained the usual assortment of pens, tape, and pads of yellow Post-It notes. She reached into the back of the drawer and pulled paper clips and dusty business cards forward. She organized the pads, threw the cards away, rubber-banded the pens. Wiped out the dust with a tissue.

Both the left- and right-hand bottom drawers were empty; apparently they had held hanging files that someone had removed. The last drawer's contents surprised her. She pulled the items out and lined them on the desk. Four snack-sized bags of licorice nibs, two high-energy bars, a Tom Clancy novel, and three packages of Sno Balls. He ate junk food! She had never seen Paul eat a Sno Ball. She couldn't imagine him doing so, especially at work, with his white shirts and good ties; it would be impossible to bite into one without getting pink coconut everywhere. She squeezed one of the packages delicately, feeling the give of the round cake, listening to the crackle of the wrapper.

There was a knock at the door, and Paul's paralegal, Andrea, entered. "Hi, Miriam."

"Hey. Come in." She had forgotten that Andrea was pregnant. Miriam's hand involuntarily went to her own stomach.

"Anything I can do?"

"I'm just cleaning things out," she explained needlessly.

Andrea sat in the chair Todd had vacated. She was an attractive woman with high cheekbones and a short, stylish pixie cut. She didn't appear to have gained any weight with the pregnancy, only looked like she had a basketball stashed under her crisp yellow maternity blouse. "I never could understand how Paul could stomach those things," she said, pointing to the Sno Balls. "I actually tried one once, and it didn't have a lot of flavor."

"Not worth the calories," Miriam agreed.

"Paul could eat anything without worrying about his weight. My husband is the same way. I hate that men are like that."

"You don't look like you have to worry about weight," Miriam offered.

"Are you kidding? I'm a beached whale!"

"You don't look like it at all. How are you feeling these days?"

"Not too bad." Andrea rubbed the side of her stomach with the heel of her hand. "Third trimester. I'm tired, but at least I'm not sick like the first three months. That was the worst. But I'm homeward bound now."

"You working right up until your due date?"

"I only get three months' maternity leave and I want to spend it all with the baby. After it comes, I mean. The only bad thing about working to the very end is the nursery probably won't be ready in time. I don't have the energy to do any decorating after work. I'm hoping my mom will come next weekend to help me shop, otherwise the baby will spend its first month sleeping in a laundry basket."

Miriam swiveled back and forth in the chair. "My mom stuck me and my brothers and sister in a dresser drawer. She never could understand why someone would go to the expense of buying a bassinet." She leaned forward to toss the junk food and Clancy novel into the box, careless about her picture at the bottom.

A question suddenly occurred to her. "Andrea, do you know of a woman named Svetlana?"

Andrea furrowed her brow but said nothing.

"She was one of Paul's clients. She introduced herself to me after the funeral. I probably wouldn't have thought anything about it except she said that she wished her husband had died instead of Paul."

"She came right out and said that?"

Miriam nodded. "I guess her husband was abusive."

"Oh. I don't recognize the name, but she must've been one of Paul's *pro bono* cases."

"He did a lot of those?"

"As many as he could fit in. He didn't tell you anything about it?"

Miriam tried to hide her embarrassment that Paul hadn't trusted her with even the most cursory mention of this. "He didn't really talk about work."

"Most lawyers do some charity work, but Paul was really passionate about it. He worked for women's shelters, doing whatever they needed. Restraining orders, prosecuting domestic violence offenders, stuff like that. I admired him. It sounds like rewarding work, but in reality it's extremely frustrating. You spend hours with these women and they end up going back to their husbands anyway, sometimes right after being beaten so hard they have to be hospitalized. One or two of those cases and I would've washed my hands of the whole thing. But Paul never lost his compassion for them."

Miriam felt queasy. She rested her elbows on the desk, picturing the hallway and the single turn before the bathroom, as if mapping it out in her mind would enable her to get there in time if she needed to. "Is someone taking care of Svetlana now that Paul isn't?"

"No one from this office, I don't think. But each shelter has a round of lawyers who work with them. I wouldn't worry about her."

"Would you be willing to check on it for me? Somehow I feel like I need to know. Maybe because Svetlana took the time to come to the funeral."

"Sure. I'll ask around and give you a call."

Later that week, Miriam called Esther. Esther bred sandhill cranes for a conservation program and always had something to tell about the trials of getting the finicky birds to mate. It wasn't as easy, or as fun, as it might seem.

As Miriam listened to Esther talk about her day, she realized that she had called her friend as a test to herself, to see if she could bring herself to admit to someone else that she was pregnant. Despite Esther's talk of pregnant birds, the conversation didn't provide any natural segues for her announcement.

Finally, during a pause, Miriam took the plunge. "Have you ever gotten a false positive on a home pregnancy test?"

Over the course of trying to get pregnant since Mei was born, Esther had taken numerous tests, had even joked about buying stock in the company.

"Once or twice," she answered, "but only when I took the test too early, before my period was due. And then the results were so faint it was hard to tell what it meant. Why?"

"When you were actually pregnant, were the results undeniable?"

"Miriam." Esther's voice took on a hard edge, perhaps because Miriam's question alluded not only to her pregnancy with Mei, but also to the two others that had ended in miscarriage. "Why do you want to know?"

"I guess I was hoping that they're notorious for giving false positives."

Esther didn't reply.

Miriam could hear faint music in the background, jazz playing on her friend's stereo. "I took one and it was positive."

"Have you gone to your doctor for a blood test?"

"No, not yet. I know I should."

"When did you take the test?"

"Christmas Eve. By that time I was two weeks overdue."

"Did the results take a while to show up?"

"No, it was immediate. And the blue stripes were really dark."

"Well, then it's probably accurate. That would make you, what, six or eight weeks along?"

"I guess," Miriam said, miserably.

"So what are you going to do?"

"I don't know. Any suggestions?"

"It's not really my call."

"I know. But I'm treading water here."

"Well, maybe if you're ambivalent about having a child, you should consider an abortion."

Miriam couldn't have been more shocked if Esther had suggested that she have the baby and let them adopt it. She struggled to know how to respond. "I don't know if I'm ambivalent. I don't really know what I think or feel about it."

"Isn't that ambivalence?"

Miriam laughed. Without mirth. "I guess."

"Hang on." Esther covered the phone with her hand and through the sound of friction on the receiver, Miriam heard the deep timbre of Charles's voice. He must've been there the entire time, listening; certainly, he'd have no trouble understanding what was happening, even if he only heard half the conversation. She regretted that he knew. "Okay, I'm back," Esther said.

"I'm sorry, Esther. Maybe I shouldn't be talking to you about this."

"Why on earth not?" She sounded angry.

"Because it's unfair that I would be the one who's pregnant. It should be you and not me."

Esther didn't disagree.

After saying good-bye, Miriam called her ob/gyn. When the receptionist asked if it was for a yearly pap, she said, without emotion, "No, it's because I'm pregnant."

"What am I going to do?" she asked Figment, who had climbed onto her chest and was purring in her face. Her breasts were tender, so she pushed the kitten onto the couch next to her and turned on the television. With the volume sufficiently loud, it was difficult to think. That suited her fine.

# eight

*t*he doctor's waiting room was crowded, mostly with women and children, although there was one young man sitting in the corner with his arm around a woman who looked like she would burst open if you pricked her tight stomach with a pin. He had a nervous smile on his face. Two pregnant mothers were talking over the sound of a daytime soap opera on television while their children dashed between the chairs, playing tag. A little boy about four years old swung out his arm and hit a girl on the back of the head as he ran past, causing her pigtails to fly. She ran to her mother, screaming, and buried her face in her lap, but the woman was so engrossed in conversation, she did nothing more than absentmindedly stroke the little girl's head. A dislike for noise rose swiftly in Miriam's throat, and she was relieved to be called out of the chaos and taken back to an exam room.

She didn't mind that the doctor kept her shivering a long time in the flimsy cotton gown. When Dr. Onalasky finally got to her, he confirmed her pregnancy, poked and prodded her, scolded her for waiting so long to see him, and gave her a due date of August 21. She received all this impassively. He stepped out of the room to let her get dressed before coming back with a tote bag filled with books and brochures on everything pregnancy-related.

"Now, according to my notes," he said, taking a seat at the little desk in the corner, "the last time I saw you, you had decided to go off the pill." He looked up from her chart. It wasn't a question, but he seemed to want confirmation.

She nodded.

"So this is a planned pregnancy."

She shrugged. It seemed strange to call it that, although technically he was right.

"You don't seem very happy."

Miriam covered her eyes with one hand, fighting for control.

"Have you changed your mind? Or does your husband not want a baby?"

"No." She pushed her hair behind her ear and dropped her hand to her lap. "It's not that. He wanted a child very much. He died in December."

"Oh," he said. Rolling his chair close to her, he placed his hand on her head.

Rather than feel awkward or condescending, his touch felt to her like the comfort or blessing a priest might offer. "He never even knew," she cried, burying her face.

The doctor rolled back to his desk and handed her a box of tissue. "Have you considered counseling or a grief support group?"

She blew her nose. "No."

"Can I give you a few numbers?"

She rolled her eyes.

"Okay," he said kindly. "I'll write them down and you'll have them when you're ready." He scribbled on a note pad. "There are plenty of people who are single parents, and there are lots of resources and support available to them. But you also have the option to terminate the pregnancy." He handed her the piece of paper. "I wrote down the number of a women's clinic I recommend."

She nodded, looking down at the note without seeing it.

"I tried to write it so you could actually read my writing."

She attempted a smile.

He helped her up and walked her down the hall. "Regardless of what you decide, come back in four weeks to see me."

She tucked the tote under her arm and pulled her coat tight before stepping back into the waiting room.

Without consciously deciding to do so, she drove to Steven's, where she found him in his studio. It was a small barnlike structure in his backyard, where a broken-down outbuilding had once stood. She had designed the space for him, filling it with windows, custom work areas of varying heights, and beautifully handcrafted cupboards to hide as much clutter as he could produce.

The clatter of the sewing machine masked her entry, and she slipped off her coat without his noticing. The room smelled of new fabric and moist, warm air from the whirring machine. She breathed deeply, feeling suddenly as if she could sleep forever, perhaps even without dreaming.

The chair Steven was working on perched on a low table, naked and exposed. Miriam touched the springs that had already been tied tight. The sewing machine shuddered to a halt, and there was a metallic clack as Steven raised the foot that held the fabric in place beneath the needle. He turned for his scissors and saw her. He yelped, clutching his head dramatically. "Oh my God, Miriam," he groaned. "You're the second person who's done that to me today."

"You shouldn't sit with your back to the door."

"I know. It's a really shitty design," he said, waving his hand to indicate the entire room.

She laughed.

"What're you up to?" he asked, getting up to give her a hug, leaving stray pieces of thread and fabric fuzz on her shirt when he pulled away.

"Could I just be here while you work?"

He didn't seem to find the request unusual. "Sure," he said, moving back to his table, where he began unwrapping fabric from a bolt and spreading it flat so he could cut it.

Set apart from his work area by a lowered ceiling, recessed lighting, and a large Asian rug was a cozy seating area where Steven could sit with clients. Along the length of one wall, squares of sample fabric hung in thick rows, and a couch and two armchairs clustered around a coffee table. The couch was one he had found at a flea market and then recovered with gold, knobby material that she told him was just begging to be covered in plastic. She had napped on it before and knew it would leave little pockmarks on any exposed skin. She pulled a blanket from one of the chairs and lay down.

Steven paused his cutting to cough alarmingly. Miriam wondered if he had seen the doctor for that yet. She'd ask later. For now, she felt as if her limbs were sinking by degrees into the couch, and she exhaled a long, deep breath before falling asleep and beginning to dream.

"Children, open the windows. Quickly." The urgency in Sister Bella's voice made second-grader Miriam go cold.

There was a commotion in the hallway, shouting, and the sound of a door slamming, and when Sr. Bella grasped the doorknob to investigate, she jumped back, shaking her hand in apparent pain. Tentatively touching the door itself, she spun toward the class, her black dress swirling around thick ankles.

"Open the windows!"

That's when the smell hit. Fire! Miriam was swept to her feet and pressed against the glass as everyone surged forward. She caught their panic and struggled to open the window, several more hands reaching out to help, and as soon as the frame scraped upward, there was another surge, and she felt the mesh of the screen pressing hard against her shoulder and face. It popped off, tumbling in slow motion to the ground, two floors below.

Adults and school children gathered outside, mouths open as they craned their necks to watch the second floor. Something flashed out of the corner of Miriam's eye, and she saw children were jumping from the windows of her brother Vinny's class. She strained forward as far as she could, searching for a glimpse of him, even calling his name as the heat intensified against her back.

"Jump!" they screamed, and Miriam thought she heard her brother calling her name, though she couldn't be sure. A boy next to Miriam pushed her roughly aside and jumped, arms helicoptering all the way down. When it felt as though her calves and back were blistering through her clothes, she jumped. Landing at an angle, her left heel made contact with the ground first, with the rest of her body following. Her leg crumpled underneath her like an accordion. Faces crowded around, blocking her view of the sky. Someone grasped her by the shoulders, another her heels, to move her out of the way, and she screamed before losing consciousness.

Ka-cha. Ka-cha. Ka-cha. She woke to the sound of Steven stapling material onto the back of the chair, rich blue brocade with a hint of roses shimmering in the background.

"You okay?" He stopped stapling and watched her closely.

"Uh huh."

"You cried out just now."

The dream, as always, had been so vivid that she awoke with the scent of smoke clinging to her. In the past she had been known to get out of bed and prowl the house, searching for flames, just to convince herself that the smell wasn't real.

"I was dreaming about the fire. About Vinny."

"Ah." He nodded, brow furrowed, and went back to his work. Not moving a muscle, she watched his confident movements through half-closed eyes.

After the fire, when she woke, she had been alone. White walls, white lights, white sheets and blanket. The color of fear. Slowly, she'd registered the ache coursing through her body, a distant hum growing louder, and a thirst so profound she thought she might not be able to pry her tongue from the roof of her mouth. A line had been attached to her left arm, held in place with thick, white tape, and her muscle tingled unpleasantly with cold where the solution entered. Her left leg was somehow immobilized, hidden beneath a tented sheet.

After what seemed like days, when the bees were fully awake in her veins, swarming furiously in her leg, a nurse appeared, hands busy and voice cheerful, asking if she wanted something to drink, warning that she could have only a little bit since she had been in surgery and didn't need an upset stomach on top of everything else. Miriam accepted gratefully the sip of water from a bendable straw that the nurse held steady for her. While the nurse checked under the

tent—Miriam didn't find out until later that her leg had broken in three places and the jagged end of her thigh bone had
punctured the skin—Miriam cried silently, gripping the
sheet in tight fists. The nurse noticed and with her bare
hands wiped away the tears rolling down Miriam's temple
and into her ears, tenderly. She stayed until Miriam fell back
into sleep.

The next time she surfaced, Steven was sitting next to her,
his head resting against the railing of her bed. At the sight
of him, she sobbed, loudly this time, while he bent over the
frame of the bed, trying to cradle her.

"Where's Vinny?" she finally asked, afraid, for some
reason, to ask for either of her parents.

"He got hurt, too."

Miriam looked past Steven to the empty bed near the
window. "But he's not in the hospital?"

"No. He was hurt too much."

She knew, despite the regular shots for pain, how much
she hurt, and thought that her brother must be in terrible
trouble if he was hurt even more than she. She kept her
worry for him to herself. Steven helped her sip some orange
juice before she once more drifted off, and after that, he was
with her in the hospital every day. They colored and listened
to the radio, and he helped her with the homework he collected from the new school she would be going to after her
leg healed.

Later, as an adult, she thought it was probably a blessing
that she kept silent in her confusion, that she had been so
slow to comprehend her brother's death.

"After the school fire, when I got out of the hospital, you never went back to college, did you, Steven?"

Finished stapling, he stretched, arching his back and kneading his neck muscles. He collapsed into one of the armchairs and put his feet on a stack of samples on the coffee table. His hair was wispy and slightly mussed. "What made you think of that?"

"I was so young, I had no idea what you were giving up to be with me."

"I have no regrets," he said, smiling at her.

"Whenever I dream about it, I swear I can smell smoke."

"I'm not surprised. I don't know if you ever get over an experience like that."

The sun was beginning to go down, and shadows inside were lengthening. Steven hunkered down in the chair so he could lean his head back. Then he folded his hands on his belly and sighed heavily.

"Mom and Dad didn't come to visit me, did they?"

"Only Mom. And then only once."

Miriam remembered her mother's visit. She had brought chocolate chip cookies in a paper bag with the top folded precisely two times and a rosary so Miriam could pray. Miriam had held very still, trying not to even blink, because if she spoke or moved, she thought her mother might disappear like a ghost.

"I could've killed her," Steven said, quietly.

Miriam looked at him sharply. His eyes were closed. "You threw the rosary away. That made a big impression on me."

He opened one eye. "In a bad way?"

She had to think about that. "No, I don't think so. I still remember what you told me. That I could say whatever I wanted to God in my own words and he would hear me just fine. Do you still believe that?"

"It killed me how scared you were. And I thought that was all you needed, to be afraid of God, too, like he had done this to you because you hadn't prayed enough and that someday something worse would happen if you didn't start praying the right way." He pushed the pile of samples with his heel and they splayed out. "But nothing I did or said could help your fear."

"Maybe that wasn't your job."

"No," he said, emphatically. "It was Mom and Dad's. But they weren't there."

"What I mean is, you were already doing so much. And having you there did make a huge difference." In the silence that followed, she wondered if that's really what she meant. Perhaps that there was nothing he or anyone else, even the best of parents, could have done to allay her fears. Or that the fact that her parents were busy burying her brother meant they could be forgiven. "What I mean is," she paused, picking at the blanket, "I'm pregnant."

Steven pulled his feet off the coffee table and sat up straight. "You are?"

She nodded.

He leaned forward on his knees, mouth open. His face registered surprise, amazement, other emotions she couldn't identify. He fell back into the chair and laughed. A rolling, until-the-end-of-your-breath belly laugh that filled the air around them. "You're pregnant?" he guffawed, and although she didn't know exactly why he was laughing, she couldn't help joining in. Soon they were both writhing, gasping for air, calming slowly, and then ratcheting up again when the other barked.

"Oh my," Steven choked out finally, swiping at his eyes. "I'm going to be a grandpa."

The feeling that came after such deep laughter, Miriam found, was not unlike crying.

nine

"*i*'m pregnant," Miriam announced with difficulty, realizing

that practice wasn't making it any easier to say. "I thought

you should know."

Martha, who had been describing in animated detail her new job at a library reference desk, fell silent. Henry had gotten tired of listening to her talk and wasn't on the phone anymore.

"Why didn't Paul say something before this?" Martha asked, after a moment.

"Because he didn't know."

"You didn't tell him?"

Martha's question was so full of hurt, Miriam overlooked the accusation. "I didn't know, either, until recently," she said wearily.

Martha began to weep.

"Why're you crying, Mom?" Miriam asked. "I thought you'd be happy."

"I'm sorry. I should be happy. I shouldn't be crying."

"No, it's okay to cry. I just don't understand."

Martha blew her nose. "Paul didn't know he was going to be a father? That's so sad."

"Maybe . . ." Miriam said hesitantly, "maybe it's better that in his last few minutes he didn't know what he was going to miss."

"Anyway," Martha said, rousing herself. "It's a blessing. We'll have something to remember him by, right?"

Miriam didn't feel up to responding to that. "Do you want to call Dad back to the phone so I can tell him?"

Martha set the phone down, and Miriam heard her calling to Henry as she moved to the next room.

When he picked up, the sound of the television blared loudly. "You're pregnant?" he cried over the noise. "Martha, turn off the TV, I can't hear myself think." It sounded like a crime drama. Sirens, yelling, gunshots. "Oh, for crying out loud, hold on." He cussed a few times before apparently finding the mute button. In the resulting silence, his response was swift and unexpected. "Is it a boy?"

Miriam stammered.

"You seen the doctor yet?"

"Well, yes, but—"

"They can figure these things out nowadays, you know. How soon before you find out?" He was like a kid in a candy store.

"I don't know—"

"We should have you visit. Martha's got a friend who can tell by reading tea leaves or some stupid thing like that—"

"She dangles a crystal over your belly," Martha interrupted, "and if it swings one way, it's a boy, and if it swings the other, it's a girl."

"Oh, right. Whatever. Point is, she's always right."

"I'm sure I'll find out when they do an ultrasound," Miriam offered.

"When's that scheduled?"

"It's not yet. But I see the doctor again in a few weeks."

"It's Paul's, right?"

It took a moment for the question to sink in. When it did, Miriam gave an enraged cry.

"Okay, okay," he said, placatingly. "Just checking. Wow. This is amazing. If it's a boy. Martha, wouldn't that be great?"

"And if it's a girl?" Miriam managed to ask.

"Then there's no one to carry on the family name," he explained, as if she should have known. "Nah, I feel it already. A grandson."

Miriam could picture the look of satisfaction on his face. It had been the same when he clapped Paul on the back after his commencement, saying with pride, "My son. The lawyer."

"You call us when you find out the sex," Henry said, concluding the conversation.

Miriam set the phone back on its stand, gently, and then looked around for something to break.

Saturday, she had lunch with Theresa. When Miriam called to suggest it, her sister had said brightly, "We can make it a tradition, lunch with my sister. But let's make it brunch, instead."

They sat at the table in Theresa's kitchen, where the windows overlooked a small pond and another house similar to all the others in the area. Each structure differed only in orientation and type of siding. Someday the trees would mature and shield the windows from neighbors' eyes, but for now each home sat exposed on its acre plot, conspicuous and, Miriam always thought, slightly embarrassed.

"That one," Theresa pointed, noticing where Miriam was looking. "Foreclosed. They only lived there eight months. Moved out from the city."

"Wow. I didn't know that could happen so fast. I thought banks didn't loan more than you could afford."

"They're probably getting a divorce. Most people can't afford one of these places without a dual income."

"That's so awful." Miriam was glad Paul had chosen to buy the modest house he did. In a good neighborhood, despite the cookie-cutter architecture, and something she could afford on her own, for a while at least.

"They furnished the place entirely with Ethan Allen. I'll let you know when they have their moving sale."

"Theresa!" Miriam scolded, laughing.

Theresa put the teapot on the table, and Miriam chose a mug from the cupboard.

"Did they have any kids?" Miriam asked.

"Two. You feeling sorry for people you don't even know?"

This was said in a bantering tone of voice, but felt like a jab. "No, actually, I was thinking that if they had kids and did have a garage sale, I might be interested in their baby stuff."

"You have a friend who's having a baby?" Theresa took a bite from a perfectly triangular blueberry scone.

"No." Miriam watched her sister chew, enjoying the fact that Theresa was, for once, slow to understand. She buttered her own scone, scattering crumbs off her plate.

Theresa's expression changed as the realization hit her. "You?" she said, incredulously. "You're pregnant?"

"Bingo."

Theresa put down her scone, wiped her lips with a napkin. When she spoke, her voice was hard. "Are you going to keep it? Are you out of your mind?"

"Do you mean, am I crazy? Delusional?" Miriam said, defensively, intentionally misunderstanding. "You mean, did I dream up this scheme in order to get sympathy?"

"I mean, what were you thinking?"

"Let's see. I was hoping that we would make a baby, that Paul would die, and that I would get to be a single mother."

Theresa stalked to the refrigerator, pulled out a carton of orange juice, slammed open a cupboard, and grabbed two glasses. At the table, she poured, sloshing juice over the side of the glass and onto her hand.

Miriam leaned back in her chair, crossing her arms angrily, almost hoping Theresa would say something else so they could go on fighting. It felt like releasing steam from a vent.

Theresa sat back in her chair, sucking juice off her fingers and then wiping them on her jeans. She took in a breath as if she were going to say something, then let it out and eyed Miriam. "Here," she said, handing her a glass of juice. When Miriam didn't reach out to accept it, she set the glass down gently in front of Miriam's plate.

Despite herself, Miriam's eyes filled with tears.

"Oh, God, Miriam, I'm sorry."

Miriam wiped at her cheeks, feeling Theresa watch her.

"You're kind of in a pickle, aren't you?"

"You might say that."

"So what are you going to do?"

"Steven wants me to move in with him."

"Oh, yeah?"

"So I won't have to worry about finances. Also to give the baby a father figure."

"Is he the kind of father figure you'd want?"

"Because he's gay?"

"Yes, there is that."

"He was a father figure to me."

"Regardless," Theresa rolled her eyes. "Who's to say you won't find another husband? People remarry, and you're still young."

Miriam laughed.

Theresa waved her hand. "You do have another choice, you know. This is the twenty-first century. Women don't have to use coat hangers anymore."

It was Miriam's turn to stare.

"Oh, come on," Theresa bit into her scone again. "Don't look so horrified."

"But you're Catholic. You're raising three million dollars for your parish."

"What's that got to do with anything?"

"Isn't that a contradiction? To be so active in the church, and then to be sitting here, suggesting I get an abortion?"

"That's a naïve way of looking at the world. Look at how fast science and technology change. Every year, we understand more, we can DO more. And look at how slowly the church policies change. We're not illiterate peasants who need to be told how to tie our shoes anymore. Sometimes we've got to use the common sense God gave us."

"Yeah, but you're talking about a view of human life that's not going to change no matter how much technology does. If anything, technology is confirming that life begins early on."

"I'm not saying abortion is an ideal solution. I wish no woman ever had to consider, let alone choose it. But when our backs are up against a wall, at least we've got the option."

Miriam busied herself gathering the crumbs around her plate into a little mound.

"You were on the pill before you got pregnant, right?"

"Yes," Miriam said in surprise.

"The church doesn't advocate that, either, does it? For the same reasons they don't advocate abortion."

Miriam pushed her hair behind her ears. Theresa was right.

Theresa's voice softened. "Look, I'm not trying to tell you what to do. I'm just saying that if you decide to get rid of it, I'll go with you. You won't have to do it alone."

To ward off tears, Miriam picked up her scone and took a bite, but immediately regretted it. Butter packed against the roof of her mouth. She hastily put down the pastry and turned inward, concentrating on holding herself absolutely still.

"You okay?"

She shook her head slightly, not daring to speak. Luckily the bathroom was close. But her stomach settled without her moving from the table, and she found she could breathe again. She wiped her upper lip, which was damp with perspiration.

"You know, there's always adoption, too," Theresa continued after Miriam sipped her tea tentatively. "There's a ton of great couples out there who're dying to have kids."

"Can you imagine what everyone would think if they saw me carrying the baby to term, only to give it up?"

Theresa shrugged, as if she could care less what others thought.

It was hard not to take this personally. "Why do you assume I can't keep the baby?"

"I don't assume anything. You just need to be realistic. Your situation isn't ideal. The baby won't have a father. You'll have to work." She ticked the items off on her fingers. "You'll have to put the kid in day care, which really means you'll be paying someone else to raise your child. You'll be completely on your own."

"All right," Miriam put her hand up. "I admit it. My situation stinks."

"At least labor for you will be easier than it was for me," Theresa said, apparently trying for a lighter tone. "I wish I could've had an epidural. Take my advice. Call ahead and reserve plenty of drugs. There's no shame in making the pain go away."

When Miriam went into the foyer to get her coat, she found Ben sitting on the stairs, reading a history textbook. He had his coat over his knees, a stocking cap pulled low over his forehead.

"I didn't know you were home," Miriam said, bumping against his shoulder as she sat on the step next to him in order to pull on her winter boots. She had taken to wearing the clumpy boots with grippy tread everywhere. When she bought them, Paul had teased that she'd need to go to Alaska to break them in. But they made her less afraid of falling.

Theresa reached through the railing and tugged at Ben's shirt. "He came home to do laundry," she said. "You must be done, though, because you look like you're going somewhere."

"I thought I'd hitch a ride to Miriam's."

"Don't you think you should ask first instead of assuming that's how Miriam wants to spend her afternoon?"

"It's okay," Miriam intervened. "I'd be glad for the company."

"What do you want at Miriam's house?" Theresa pressed.

"I want to work on the canoe."

"Don't overstay your welcome. I'll come get you later so Miriam doesn't have to bother."

"It wouldn't be a bother." Miriam held out her hand, pulled him to his feet. On weekends and over winter breaks, when it was too cold for basketball in the driveway, he and Paul had worked on the canoe together. Since they were using no power tools, the only sounds that drifted out of the basement were their voices and the occasional shout of laughter. She had learned not to ask Paul what they talked about, because he would merely shrug and say he couldn't remember. She couldn't tell if this was his way of pleading the fifth in order to keep Ben's confidence, or if he was telling the truth, that he really couldn't remember.

If it were anyone but Ben walking into the house with her, she would be embarrassed by the state of things. Dirty dishes strewn around, blankets and pillows bunched on the couches in both the family and living rooms where she had fought off sleepless nights, unopened mail in piles on the floor by the front door. She had received the bill for the emergency room visit and decided that the mail was best left for another, stronger time.

Ben followed her almost apologetically into the kitchen, head down and hands in his pockets, making no move toward the basement where the canoe was. He declined her offer of coffee or tea. Rather than sit and stare at one another, she cast about for something to do.

"You want to help me?" she asked. "There's some stuff in the attic I need to get rid of, but I've been too chicken to go up there on my own."

"I'll get the ladder," he said, gratefully, heading to the garage.

The entrance to the attic was just outside the door of the guest bedroom, near the top of the stairs.

Once he had retrieved the ladder, Ben took the stairs two at a time, knocking it against the wall, oblivious to the scuff marks he left behind.

"You want me to climb up there?" he asked, peering up at the square hole in the ceiling.

"No, I want to make sure everything's in good condition for when I sell the house."

"You going to move?"

"Yeah," she said, slowly, to let her thoughts catch up to her words. "I think I am. I've never really liked this house all that much. You're the first to know, so don't go spreading it around."

"Your secret's safe with me."

She climbed the paint-splattered rungs while Ben held the ladder steady. Pushing the wooden cover up and out of the way, she climbed halfway into the attic, pausing to let her eyes adjust to the gloom. It was chilly, though not so cold that she could see her breath.

A boardwalk, sticky with dust, extended the length of the house, marking a path through thick yellow insulation. Above what she estimated to be the bathroom, the insulation looked wet and moldy. She decided to ignore this.

Clustered nearby were grocery sacks overflowing with paper. She hefted herself all the way up, legs flailing slightly. Ben climbed the ladder to accept each bag she handed down.

"What is all this?" he grunted.

"It's Paul's brilliant filing system. Mostly old school papers and lecture notes, I think."

She backed out of the attic feet first and felt Ben's hands guiding her safely to the top rung. Together, they dragged the bags into the office and settled on the floor. She was right about the contents of the bags, and her stomach lurched at the familiar scrawl of handwriting in each notebook.

"Look at this," she said, handing over an English paper for one of Paul's undergrad classes, titled "Virginia Wolfe at the Lighthouse." It had received a D. The professor had scrawled in red: "Do not play with font size and margins to make the paper seem longer," and "Who is this 'Virginia Wolfe', anyway?"

Miriam laughed.

"Why on earth did he keep this?" Ben asked.

"I would've burned it in shame the moment I got it back from the teacher." Miriam thought for a moment. "Actually, I never would've turned in something like that in the first place."

"My mom would kill me if I got a grade like this."

"Maybe that's not a bad thing. Paul was never too concerned with grades. Or what his parents thought. I think he figured he was in college and that was good enough."

Ben flipped through the paper, shaking his head. "I would've thought Uncle Paul would do better than this."

"He did a lot of partying as an undergrad. You don't know anything about that kind of thing, do you?"

"Who, me? Of course not," he smirked, before turning serious again. "I've never gotten a D, though."

"Paul didn't really buckle down and start studying until he got to law school," she said, flipping through a notebook filled with lecture notes on criminal law. "At least that's what he told me." She held the notebook open for Ben to see. Paul had doodled a waterfall over the entire page, complete with spray, jumping fish, and jagged rocks at the bottom. A kayak halfway down the page was spilling out a cartoonish man who was upside down, with "yaaaa-hooooo" coming from his gaping mouth.

"I guess he learned a lot during that lecture," Ben quipped.

Miriam tore that page out of the notebook and set it aside, but found nothing else she wanted to keep. Ben gathered all the paper into large garbage bags while she went through the last binder. She gasped when she opened it.

"What is it?" Ben asked.

"Sketches," she said, leafing slowly through the pages. "Houses I designed."

Ben tossed a full garbage bag into the hall then moved close to look over her shoulder. "You did those?"

"Yeah, but I always threw them away." Most of the drawings were done in pencil, but she had taken the time to add color and landscaping to some. Each was an exploded diagram that showed the layout of each floor as well as a front and side angle of the house.

"Those are pretty good," Ben observed.

"I can't believe he saved all these." She smoothed her hand over one sketch that she remembered crumpling in frustration, feeling the creases in the paper against her palm.

"Uncle Paul told me once that he wished you would go back to school and study architecture."

"He did?"

Ben shrugged. "Have you thought about it?"

"Not really. I couldn't go back to school."

"Because you can't afford it?"

"No, it's not that. It's just unrealistic. A dream. Especially now that—" She stopped herself.

"Now that you're having a baby?"

She looked at him sharply. "How'd you know that?"

"I heard you and Mom talking."

"You did?" she said, weakly.

"I think you shouldn't be so afraid to do what you want, Aunt Miriam. Forget my mom and everyone else. What do you want?"

Miriam blinked. "Who are you," she said, "and what have you done with my nephew?"

## ten

"*M*iriam." Father Jake's voice through the answering machine skewered Miriam to the couch. She muted the television and willed her heart to stop pounding. She had managed to avoid him completely since she and Steven met with him about the funeral, when she had told him that they would not be having a religious service.

"I keep replaying our last conversation in my head, when I tried to convince you to go against Henry's wishes for the funeral. I'm regretting that now," he said.

Miriam was surprised. Naïve as it was, it had never occurred to her that a priest would have regrets.

He sighed, a fluttery sound through the phone. "Henry put you in an impossible situation, and I want you to know that I can understand why you did what you did." He paused and Miriam imagined he was swiveling back and forth in his office chair, as he sometimes did when he was thinking. "If you need to talk," he concluded, "or if you just need someone to sit with you, I'm here."

She had thought of calling him a million times. Once again she decided to straighten the house rather than think about it now.

On the kitchen counter was the bag of information the doctor had given her. She cracked open *What to Expect When You're Expecting* for the first time, looking in the index for "teeth." Maybe there was a logical explanation for why she nearly puked every time she brushed her teeth. It wasn't the taste of the toothpaste; she'd tried using a dry brush, which didn't help. Maybe there was something about the motion that triggered vomiting. Ah, there it was: *teeth, in pregnancy.* She flipped to the page and read: "The gums, like the mucous membranes of the nose, become swollen, inflamed, and tend to bleed easily because of pregnancy hormones." Nice.

She shoved the book back in the bag, noticing as she did the piece of paper on which Dr. Onalasky had written phone numbers. She studied the name of the woman's clinic, the contact name for the grief support group. Folding the note into a small square, she tucked it into her pocket and threw everything else away; this felt good, like unburdening herself. She scoured the house, finding things in every room she could likewise toss. Magazines, Christmas cards, CDs she'd never listen to again, the few remaining items from her mother's house she no longer felt sentimental about.

As she hoisted the full garbage bags into the garage, she felt like an addict, wishing she and Paul had collected more useless items over the years, just so she could feel the pleasure of throwing them away.

There were some things that however much she hated them she had to keep. Like the pillow on the living room couch with glittery, embroidered angels. She had once made the mistake of telling Theresa how much she liked a certain popular painting of three cherubic angels—the colors were so warm, deep reds and golds, the angels so pleased-looking. Nearly every birthday and Christmas since then, Theresa had given her angelic gifts. Posters, candles with wings embossed in the wax and little halos perched above the wick, figurines, stained-glass window hangings.

Figment stuck his head in the room and meowed hungrily. "What else can we do to make this day pass?" Miriam asked him, getting up to check his food dish. It was empty, and she couldn't remember the last time she had fed him. She stroked his back, feeling him arch under her fingers.

"I'm sorry, kitty," she said guiltily, watching as he pounced on his food. Back at the couch, she lay with her head on an angel and drifted into a fitful sleep where dreams awaited.

She found herself on an unfamiliar street corner, waiting for a bus that she felt certain she had already missed, her anxiety like a terrible itch she couldn't quite locate. She strained to see through the heavy traffic, checking her watch obsessively, although she didn't know what time the bus was due.

When a diesel rumble and a flash of cloudy windows told her the bus was coming, she felt sweaty with relief. She dug in her pocket for change, bumping against pedestrians, and stepped toward the curb. The bus coughed out puffs of soot as the driver changed gears, speeding up rather than slowing down. It started to pass by, and Miriam waved her arms frantically until she saw Paul sitting in the back seat, his head angled slightly away. He didn't see her.

"Wait," she screamed, running alongside his window. "I need to talk to you." But the bus pulled away, swallowed up in traffic, and Paul never looked in her direction or heard her cries. She stood alone on a suddenly empty street, coughing from the dark exhaust the bus had left behind.

Miriam woke with a start when Figment jumped onto the couch next to her, and she closed her eyes tight, acutely disappointed to find her limbs intact. Amputation would be better than this.

A new sound snuck into her awareness, slowly, coming from outside. This one was real, not dreamed: the scrape of a solitary shovel against the sidewalk. She had to force herself to peek through the curtains to see who it was, hating herself for the ridiculous hope that it was Paul.

But it was Steven, shoveling the driveway. At least three inches of snow, light and fluffy, covered everything, softening the lines of the neighborhood. She let the curtain drop back into place and retreated to the bathroom, where nausea demanded her attention for a time.

She was in the entryway, waiting and still trembling when Steven let himself in, his familiar cough preceding him.

"Hey," he said, shucking off his boots and leaning down to pull his right sock back up. "It snowed." He pulled off his stocking cap, his hair crackling with static. "It's supposed to get into the thirties later today, so the snow probably would've melted on its own, but in case it freezes tonight, I didn't want it to melt on the sidewalk and then turn to ice."

Miriam took his coat and smoothed the hair sticking up over his ears. "You want some tea?"

"Sure." He breathed into his cupped hands and rubbed them together vigorously. "Something hot sounds good."

The kettle felt substantial in her hand as she filled it with water.

"You want me to start a fire?" Steven asked, standing in front of the empty fireplace.

"If you want."

By the time the water boiled and the green tea had steeped to a rich, summery color, a fire was crackling and spitting out heat.

Steven accepted the mug gratefully, but didn't sit down.

She sat in a chair, pulling her legs under her. The tea smelled and tasted good, for once. As she watched her brother shifting his weight in front of the fire, Miriam realized he wasn't just trying to get warm, he was nervous.

"What's up?" she asked, hoping he wasn't working up his nerve to run through the warning signs for clinical depression or something else that would put her on the spot.

"Oh, boy," he said, perching on the couch and staring into the flames. He sipped his tea hastily and grimaced. "I don't know how to say this."

Miriam tried to imagine what would be so hard for him to say, but came up blank. A spark popped out of the fireplace and glowed briefly on the floor. When he still didn't speak, she prompted him. "Steven, you're starting to scare me. Spit it out."

"Right." His eyes flicked toward her and away. "I've met someone."

"You've met someone?" she repeated in disbelief, as much from surprise that this was the cause of his discomfort as from the feeling that she, in fact, didn't really want to hear this. "But that's great," she said evenly. "Why would you be afraid to tell me?"

"Well, you know," he said, significantly.

"No," she shook her head, mystified.

"The timing is so bad."

"Because?" she asked, confused.

"It's so soon after Paul."

"What does the one have to do with the other?"

"I keep thinking about how I felt after Sean died. The last thing I wanted was to see other couples in love. It was too painful."

She swallowed, pressing her thumb along a seam on the arm of the leather chair she was sitting in. The stitches were rough.

"So you're in love?" she asked, softly.

"Ridiculous, isn't it? At my age." He rubbed the back of his head, causing his hair to stand out again. "I don't know what I'm thinking, to be honest."

"How'd you meet?"

"At a poetry slam."

She laughed. "You went to a poetry slam?"

He laughed with her, rolling his eyes. "You remember Tim?"

She nodded. Tim was a teenager who lived near Steven and whose parents were going through a messy divorce. He sometimes brought his homework to Steven's studio, where he could work in peace, and the two had struck up a friendship.

"Tim's been going to these poetry slams, and he invited me to come see him. It was amazing; those kids get up there and pour their hearts out." Steven shook his head as if to get himself back on track. "Anyway, I was the oldest one in the room by at least thirty years and was slinking around, trying to not make a fool of myself when I bumped into Joseph."

"You thirty years older than him, too?"

Steven laughed at this. "No, he's the same age as me. He's the one who got the poetry slams started, though now he lets the kids run the whole show. He's a poet."

"Ah," she said. "Is that code for 'not self-sufficient'?"

"You're worse than a father!" Steven grinned. "Next you'll be asking him what his intentions are."

"Maybe I will." Miriam matched his expression.

"He's gainfully employed, I promise. He teaches high school English. Helps kids get involved in creative writing and poetry slams as a way to give them something positive to do. Keep them off drugs and all that jazz." He got up to throw another log on the fire.

"How long have you been seeing him?"

"Almost six months," Steven said.

Miriam stared into her mug. A piece of Figment's fur floated on top of the liquid. She fished it out. He had been seeing Joseph for quite a while before Paul died, so clearly something else had kept him from telling her about their relationship. "Well," she said, not knowing whether to press him about this. "I'm glad you finally told me."

"I—"

The phone interrupted him. Miriam didn't move to pick it up.

"You going to get that?"

"And disturb Figment?" she said. The cat was a warm lump on her lap.

Theresa's voice sounded tinny, filtered through the answering machine. "Miriam. Have you made the appointment with Planned Parenthood, like we talked about?"

Steven's head swung toward Miriam, his mug halted in front of his chin.

"I still want to go with you, but I need to get it on my calendar. Plus, the sooner for you, the better." Theresa paused, then added: "Oh, and I've got a Web site for you to look at. *Catholic Choices.* Or, no, wait. *Choices for Catholics.*

Something like that. I'll look it up again and give you the address. I think it'll help."

The brief dial tone and click of the answering machine sounded emphatic.

Steven continued to study Miriam. "I can think of only one reason you'd go to Planned Parenthood and not your regular doctor."

She shrugged, avoiding his eyes.

"Miriam," he said, his voice pleading. "Please don't do anything rash."

"I'm thinking of selling this house. Would that be rash?"

"No, because you can come live with me. I wasn't being glib when I suggested it before."

"Some would say that selling your house barely two months after becoming a widow is hasty. You want some more tea?" She pushed Figment off her lap and went into the kitchen. The burner clicked several times before it caught.

"I'm serious, Miriam." Steven had followed her.

"I know you are. But I don't see how I could move in with you. What about Joseph?"

"He's not living with me."

"Yet."

Steven put his fists to his forehead in frustration. "See, that's one of the reasons I hated to tell you about him, why the timing is so bad. I didn't want you to think he's more important to me than you and your baby are. You've got to believe me."

"I do believe you. But maybe I shouldn't be more important than him. At what point do you stop putting your life on hold for me?"

"I'm not doing that. This is what family is for. Joseph understands that."

"You've talked to him about me?"

"How could I not?"

"He knows I'm pregnant?"

Steven stepped around the kitchen counter and retrieved his mug from the coffee table in the family room. He brought it back and put it in the sink.

Miriam didn't want more tea after all. She snapped off the burner and leaned against the counter, arms crossed.

Steven turned toward her. "Just promise that you'll consider it, okay? We can figure this out together. I know we can."

"Okay," she acquiesced, allowing him to pull her into a tight hug.

His apparent relief told her that he took her "okay" to mean she wouldn't have an abortion. She didn't clarify, partly to avoid hurting him and partly because she was at such a loss herself.

After he left, she listened to Theresa's message once more before deleting it. She longed to talk to Father Jake: To confess her sins to him and hear him say, ". . . may God give you pardon and peace. I absolve you. . . ." To ask him to pray for her since she herself was continually coming up blank.

But she knew it would be pointless, because she couldn't very well tell him everything that was weighing on her. She cringed, imagining his disapproval were he to find out that on Theresa and Esther's advice, she was considering an abortion. Father, like Steven and her in-laws, would be opposed to it, though for different reasons. She was trapped in the crossfire of their conflicting desires.

The need to do something, anything, led her back to the kitchen, where she searched through the junk drawer for the business card of the Realtor who had helped Paul buy the house. She dialed and told Suzi Engle she needed to sell.

# eleven

$S$uzi was an enthusiast who spoke in capital letters.

February was a LITTLE early in the selling season, so she couldn't promise anything right away, but soon it would be spring, which was a PERFECT time to have a house on the market, and she was sure they'd find a buyer in NO time.

Strange, hearing the Realtor talk about spring as if it were a certainty.

Because the house was well-maintained and already stripped of most clutter, it wasn't long before Suzi could slap a "for sale" sign in the ground.

Harder than getting ready to sell her house, now that the decision was made, was trying to figure out where to go once she was homeless. In the dining room, Miriam spread a map on the table; it bubbled along the crisp, new folds like unexplored mountain ranges.

Figment jumped up and sat on Oregon, his tail wrapped tightly about him. She had become lax about keeping him off the table.

"The question," Miriam said, "is where should we move? Why stay in Illinois? We could go to Oregon." She poked at his front paw and he shifted slightly. "Although it rains there all the time, doesn't it? That would be depressing."

She traced interstate highways east from Chicagoland, imagining what it would be like to pull up roots and start fresh somewhere else. Her fingertip lingered in Pennsylvania, then moved on to Massachusetts.

She crossed her arms over the map and rested her chin on her wrist, envisioning a one-room cottage on Cape Cod. Hardwood floors, a loft with a mattress on the floor, blue bedspread, white walls. Sheer curtains fluttering over an open window. Crisp and simple. The sound of surf, the smell of salt-laden air. Yes, that would be the life.

She wondered what states her father had seen on his steel-hauling routes. And if he was ever tempted to dump his load and stay put, wherever he was. She couldn't imagine he looked forward to coming home, especially after Vinny died.

Only once had he taken her for a ride in his rig. Over the sharp protests of her mother, he had beckoned her toward the open cab door and hooked his fingers under her armpits. She jumped, and he hoisted her to a ledge from which she could scramble inside. When he slammed the door shut, she was for a moment alone in her father's world, smelling of diesel and cigarettes and warm pine from a cardboard tree that hung from a knob on the dashboard. Heat pressed against her like gravity.

"Hotter than hades in here, but you'll get used to it," he said as he swung himself into the driver's seat, rolling his window down with a quick rotation of his left hand.

The familiarity with which he spoke to her, the way he used an almost-swear word in her presence, made her want to risk sitting closer to him. Her bare legs stuck to the hot vinyl seat with every scoot sideways, the rumble of the engine reverberating in her bones.

Fascinated, she watched his feet work the clutch and accelerator, his right hand moving between the enormous steering wheel and the stick shift, which vibrated and shook with a life of its own. She wanted to feel that vibration against her own palm and reached out to touch it, sensing her whole arm would tingle with its power.

Before she made contact with the hard plastic, she felt splitting pain in her left leg and heard the whack of a hand against bare skin.

"Don't EVER touch anything in here without asking!" her father roared over the engine and rush of traffic noise through the open windows.

The ghostly imprint of his fingers appeared on her thigh, and she knew better than to explain that she had only wanted to feel it, not move it. She knew not to move it. She gulped back tears.

"This is a dangerous vehicle. Someone could get killed and I got to pay attention all the time. No room for mistakes."

He had struck her bad leg, right above the scar from her surgery.

Miriam twiddled her fingers on the map, and Figment pounced at them from his position on the Pacific Northwest.

"Oh, who am I kidding?" she sighed. "There's no way I'm moving away from this area."

She reached for the printouts of houses for sale that Suzi had dropped off, rejecting them all at a glance. Too big, too boxy, too pretentious, on a street that's too busy, too much work, too this or that. She thumbed through the entire pile, though she didn't know what she wanted and had little faith she'd recognize it when she saw it.

"You serious about moving?" Esther asked over dinner.

"I'm thinking about Alaska. I'd like to sell my car and buy a snowmobile."

"Yeah, and lose your mind in the winter when it's dark twenty-four hours a day. Besides, you'd get lonely."

"I'd be doing pretty well if loneliness was my only problem." Miriam pushed a cherry tomato around her salad plate.

"You think maybe you've decided to move in order to avoid making other decisions?" Esther looked pointedly at Miriam's water glass. She had raised her eyebrows when

Miriam turned down the waiter's suggestion of a cocktail or a glass of wine.

Miriam ignored this reference to her pregnancy. "I never really liked our house. Paul bought it when we were engaged, and I didn't feel like I had the right to object." She rolled her eyes. "That stupid sauna." Esther knew about the sauna in the corner of their basement, which had struck Paul as hilariously ridiculous but at the same time seemed to be a selling point for him. Miriam could count on one hand the number of times he had actually used it.

"For some reason," she continued, "that sauna always creeped me out."

"But wherever you go, you'll be taking yourself with you."

As the waiter replaced their salad plates with great bowls of pasta, Miriam contemplated this, the notion that she herself, and not what was happening *to* her, was the enemy from which there was no escape.

"Life will still be life," Esther concluded, sadly, as if she felt the weight of this, too.

Henry called to inform Miriam that they were coming for a visit and had already purchased tickets. Non-refundable tickets. Clever, how he slipped that in.

"Really? When? I'll need to check my calendar."

"What could possibly be on your calendar?" he retorted. "You're not working. What else you got going on?"

He had a point, though she still would have preferred he go through the motion of asking if it was okay to visit.

"We want to help set up the nursery," he declared. "You can make an appointment to get an ultrasound, too, and we'll go along since you seem to be having trouble following through on that."

Miriam regretted admitting to him that she had missed her last doctor's appointment.

"That would be so much fun," Martha piped up. "They didn't have ultrasounds when I was pregnant with Paul. I've always wanted to see what that was like."

Miriam could think of very few things she'd rather *not* do than have her in-laws witness the ultrasound. It was more than a little twisted. What did they think, she was twelve?

Their impending visit added pressure to finally make a decision. Theresa's message, too, haunted her. "The sooner, the better," she had said. There wasn't a moment in which Miriam forgot that she was nearing the second trimester, when an abortion would be more difficult.

Henry and Martha would never forgive her if that's what she chose, so she'd have to tell them it was a miscarriage. She hated lying, hated her circumstances, hated the way her hand was being forced.

Restless, she gathered together a box of Paul's baseball items that she knew Henry wanted, threw it all in the car and headed to the used sporting goods store Paul had frequented.

Stepping into the store, she was immediately overwhelmed by the smell: a mixture of leather mitts and dusty cards intermingled with locker rooms and old socks. It reminded her of getting into the car on a summer day with Paul hot and sweaty from a game, his glove and cleats tossed onto the floor in the back. The air in the car would be baked hot from the afternoon sun, and they would ride with the windows all the way down, yelling to each other over the noise of wind and traffic until the air conditioner showed enough promise to let them roll the windows back up.

"Can I help you?" A man seated on a stool behind a glass counter full of baseball cards had watched her come in.

He and Paul had been on a first-name basis, she knew, and although she had been there only once, she felt disappointed that he didn't recognize her.

"I'd like to sell this," she said, putting the box on the counter. A radio buzzed with the talk of a sports channel. "If you're interested."

He stood and rummaged through the box. "Yeah, I think we can probably work something out. You want some coffee?"

She shook her head and waited while he disappeared into the back office to pour himself a cup. The walls of the store were lined with shelves overflowing with cleats, roller blades, and helmets. Bats hung in haphazard rows along with hockey sticks. It was amazing to her that Paul could disappear into this shop for hours on end, talking with the owner and other customers about whatever it was that baseball fanatics talked about. She had never paid enough attention.

He returned with a Cubs mug, which, heavy with stains, looked as if it had never been washed. She was glad she hadn't accepted his offer for a cup.

"Okay, let's see what you've got." He looked each item over carefully. "Signed jersey, pretty standard. Signed baseball, yeah, okay, that's worth a little more, but not much. Where'd you get all this anyway?"

She stammered, not having anticipated this question.

He stopped shuffling through a stack of cards to look at her.

"I'm getting ready to move," she said, finally, because that was, at least, true. "I'm cleaning out the attic."

He raised his eyebrows as though he didn't believe her, then shrugged. "So long as you're not selling your husband's stuff out from under him."

"You've had people do that?"

"After a fight, the wife comes in, sells her old man's stuff without him knowing. Next thing I know, I've got a guy in here, cussing me out and yelling about lawsuits." He paused for a slurp of coffee. "But usually that happens during baseball season when guys are glued to their TV sets. Wrong time of year for that."

"Yeah, I guess it is," she forced a smile. "No, it's nothing like that."

"Nah, you don't look like the type anyway." He turned his attention back to the box, obviously enjoying himself. The thought of an angry husband didn't seem to threaten him too much. He stuck his fingers inside Paul's glove, working it open and shut a few times. Pounded his fist into the palm.

The familiar gesture, the sound of knuckles against leather, made her want to leap over the counter and rip the glove off his hand. The cruel pleasure with which she had been contemplating handing Henry an envelope of cash when he asked for Paul's things began to ebb away.

"I think I've changed my mind," she blurted.

He looked up, surprised. "About everything?"

She pulled the glove off his hand. "I don't know."

"Well, I can tell you that altogether, this stuff is worth about fifty bucks. Probably had more sentimental value for whoever owned it."

"My husband," she admitted. "He used to come in here a lot. Paul Kovatch."

"Yeah, I know him. He gonna show up tomorrow threatening to sue?" he teased.

"He died in December."

"My God. What happened?"

"Heart attack." She hugged the mitt to her chest. "He had a heart attack shoveling snow. The first storm we had this season, a few weeks before Christmas."

"I remember that storm. Schools were cancelled, so my kid was here with me all day." He set his coffee down, shook his head. "Is Paul's old man still around?"

"Yeah, why?"

"I know they used to go to games together, is all. Thought maybe he'd like to keep this in the family."

Guilt caused her cheeks to heat up, but didn't keep her from shaking her head. "I'll keep the glove, and that's it."

He pushed a button on the cash register and it opened with a ching. He counted out one hundred dollars and held the bills out to her.

"That's more than you said."

"Yeah, well, I give different rates to friends."

Over the tinkling of the doorbell, she heard him call out, "You take care now."

She wondered how soon she would regret this little act of rebellion.

# twelve

*E*sther and Charles arrived early one morning to drop off

Mei. They were going to spend a few nights in a bed and

breakfast for their anniversary, and when Charles's parents were at the last moment unable to babysit, Miriam agreed to fill in.

Mei, who had fallen asleep on the way over, cried petulantly when they left, saying she didn't want to do any of the things Miriam offered as a distraction. Watch television, listen to music, read a book, no, no, no.

"Well," Miriam said to her where she lay on the floor, arms and legs flung wide, "I'm going to make pancakes. I would love to have you help me, but if you'd prefer to stay here instead, that's okay, too."

Mei rolled onto her stomach and made a noise of annoyance, hiding her face in the crook of her elbow, but by the time Miriam had measured all the ingredients and was stirring the batter, Mei was tugging her shirt, ready to help.

"You think we should make smiley faces on the pancakes with chocolate chips?" she asked.

"Chocolate chips?" Mei breathed, her eyes wide.

"Can you think of a reason we shouldn't have chocolate chip pancakes?"

"No, uh-uh," Mei responded quickly, clearly afraid Miriam was about to come to her senses.

Watching Mei dig into the pancakes and anticipating the sugar-high to come, Miriam herself carefully avoided the chocolate, which still brought back memories of too many martinis.

After breakfast, Miriam took Mei to a craft store, where they picked out supplies to make art projects. All the things she hadn't been allowed to waste as a little girl or make a mess with—tape, glitter glue, construction paper, stickers, pompoms, beads, ribbon, pipe cleaners. Mei squealed when she saw a bag of googly eyes and insisted on holding it, letting the bag go only long enough for the clerk to scan it.

"Googly, googly," she said over and over from her car seat, shaking the bag for emphasis, and Miriam had to admit it was a fun word to say.

On the way home, Miriam stopped at the library to stock up on books and videos, anticipating the need for backup once Mei tired of crafting. They were sitting at a table buried in piles of books Mei had grabbed from the shelves, sifting through the options and reading as they went. Mei listened intently, her face registering the ups and downs of the story, even as she worried the bag of googly eyes with her index finger, opening a corner just enough to squeeze out one of the eyes.

Miriam paused her reading to show Mei how to peel off the backing so the eye could be stuck to something.

"I think I could read a lot better if I had a third eye right here," she said, pointing to her forehead.

Soon they both had eyes stuck to their skin, and when Miriam shook her head to make it wobble, Mei shouted with laughter.

Miriam clapped her hand over the little girl's mouth, laughing, but shushing her. "We have to be quiet," she whispered conspiratorially when she saw someone moving toward them. Mei pretended to zip up her lips.

Miriam started reading again, in hushed tones.

"Miriam?"

It wasn't a librarian coming to scold them, as Miriam had thought, but Andrea, Paul's paralegal, with a baby strapped to her front. All that was visible was a dark tuft of hair, because the baby was scrunched low in the sling.

"Andrea!" Miriam exclaimed. "You had your baby!"

"Yeah." Andrea patted the baby's rump, looking pleased. "Not too long after I saw you. She came a week early."

"How'd everything go?"

"Take everything you've ever heard about how horrible labor is and multiply that by a thousand. It's indescribable.

All those women who say you forget the pain the minute they put the baby in your arms? Liars. All of them. You don't forget thirty-six hours of hell."

"Yikes," was all Miriam could think of to say.

Mei got up from her chair and leaned into Miriam, staring with wide eyes at the baby. Miriam introduced her. "Mei is staying with me for a few days while her parents have a mini-vacation, right?"

Mei nodded.

"Would you like to see baby Beth?" Andrea asked her, squatting down so Mei could peer into the sling. Andrea shifted the bundle so the top of the baby's forehead and tightly closed eyes appeared above the cloth.

Mei leaned close, studying the baby with an intent look on her face.

"When do you have to go back to work?" Miriam asked.

"Ten days," Andrea said, her smile faltering and her eyes filling with tears. "I had no idea it was going to be this hard to leave her. I feel like the Wicked Witch of the West handing my baby over to a babysitter for eight hours a day." She laughed ruefully, swiping at her eyes. "I'm sorry. I cry at the drop of a hat these days."

"No, it's all right," Miriam reassured her. "Do you have to go back?"

"My husband has been offering to figure out a way for me to stay home, but I don't know. I don't see how we can afford it."

"My mommy had a baby in her tummy," Mei announced suddenly, having finished her careful study of baby Beth.

Miriam's heart leapt at the past tense, but Andrea didn't understand the significance, because she said, "She did? That's wonderful. Is it a little brother or a little sister?"

"I don't know. It died."

Andrea looked at Miriam in shock.

"Oh, sweetie," Miriam said, putting her arm around the little girl and kissing the top of her head. She was wondering how to gracefully end the conversation with Andrea when a man approached and helped her from her crouching position.

"There you are," he said. "You ready to go?"

"My husband, Dave," Andrea explained to Miriam, laughing nervously. "I was just wondering how I was going to get off the floor." They headed toward the exit. "It was nice to see you."

Once they were out of sight, Miriam slumped back in her chair. "What do you say, kiddo? Should we get out of here?"

"Auntie Mimi?"

"Yeah?" Miriam inclined her head in Mei's direction, hoping she would be able to come up with the right words to comfort a four-year-old who was processing her mother's miscarriage.

"You have three eyes."

Miriam felt the small plastic bubble located between her eyebrows and laughed. "So I do." The entire time, Andrea had said nothing. "Might as well leave it on now. Thankfully I'm not alone." She pointed to Mei's forehead with a smile.

"Miriam." Andrea's voice caused both of them to whip around. "Sorry," she said, "I didn't mean to startle you. I forgot to mention it before, but I looked into that *pro bono* case for you. It turns out that Todd took it over. When I asked him about it, he said he wanted to do it for Paul."

"Thanks," Miriam said, trying to smile as Andrea said good-bye once more.

"Is it time for a nap yet?" Miriam asked, gathering into a pile the books they were going to check out.

"No way, hosay," Mei chimed.

"Somehow I knew you were going to say that."

The next day Miriam took Mei to McDonald's for lunch. Another brilliant idea, she thought, as Mei scrambled on her hands and knees through the plastic tubes of the Playland. The little girl had barely sat at the table long enough to eat half a cheeseburger before she dashed off, kicking her shoes across the room and diving head first into a slide to scramble the wrong way up.

Ever since the library, Miriam had waited for Mei to bring up Esther's miscarriage again. She didn't feel it was appropriate to ask any questions—if Mei needed to talk about it again, she would. Miriam felt awful that Esther hadn't said anything to her. It was true that Esther had seemed distracted and increasingly reluctant to talk about Miriam's pregnancy. This was understandable, but at some point, wouldn't she have trusted Miriam with the information?

"Look at me!" Mei cried through an opening above Miriam's head. They waved to each other and Mei's face disappeared, replaced by the blonde head of a little girl she had befriended.

"Did you adopt her?" a woman in the next booth who had two children somewhere in the maze asked.

"No, I'm watching her for a friend."

"My sister adopted a little girl from China. That's why I asked."

"Ah."

"They're beautiful, aren't they? Like little china dolls."

Miriam didn't know whether to agree out of politeness or be insulted on Mei's behalf. She gave a half-hearted smile. She took a few more sips of water and realized she had to go to the bathroom for the millionth time that day.

She corralled Mei at the bottom of a slide. Heat emanated from the top of Mei's head, her bangs clinging to her forehead.

"Come on, sweetie, let's go to the bathroom."

Mei tried to yank away, her voice raised in protest.

"We'll come back," Miriam struggled to hold onto her. The blonde stood off to the side, waiting.

"But I don't have to go," Mei wailed.

The woman who had spoken to Miriam called out from her booth. "I'll keep an eye on her. She'll be fine with my kids."

Miriam looked at Mei uncertainly, and her bladder helped make the decision. "Okay, thanks," she said, and Mei happily fled, the other girl close on her heels.

Miriam hurried, and couldn't have been gone more than five minutes, but when she returned to the play area, she was horrified to see Mei sobbing, with the woman kneeling in front of her, talking earnestly.

"What is it?" she called out, panicked. Mei ran to her. "What happened?"

The woman got up, her hands held high. "I don't know what happened, she wouldn't tell me. But I don't think she's hurt."

Miriam led Mei back to their booth and scooted in, pulling Mei with her. Mei's face was flushed, and big tears spilled down her face. Miriam helped her blow her nose and she began to calm down.

"Can you tell me what happened?"

"That girl called me a name," Mei pointed at a brunette with wispy pigtails, beginning to wail once more.

"Ssshhh, it's okay," Miriam comforted, hugging her close, but she herself didn't feel okay. She and Paul had spent enough time with the Lings to see firsthand the racism they encountered. Esther, especially, faced with ferocity the prospect of protecting Mei from such ugliness. Miriam felt sick that it had happened here, under her care.

"Sometimes people aren't very nice and they say things they shouldn't," she said, wiping Mei's nose and cheeks. "But that doesn't mean what they say is true."

Mei still cried a little bit, but Miriam could tell she was now forcing the tears along.

"What did the girl call you?"

"I was going down the slide, and she didn't wait long enough, and we bumped into each other. And she said, 'Get out of my way, buster!'"

"She called you *buster?*"

Mei nodded.

"Well," Miriam struggled to keep a straight face. "That wasn't very nice, was it?"

"Uh-uh."

"You know what? You just ignore little girls who say naughty things, okay?"

"Okay." Mei rested her arms on the table, drumming her fingers and looking around the room with renewed interest.

"Do you want to play some more, or should we go home?"

"Play!"

Miriam couldn't help it. The moment Mei was out of sight, she laughed out loud. "Everything's okay," she said to the other woman who had been shooting concerned looks in their direction.

Miriam was exhausted by the time Esther and Charles returned. They stayed only long enough to exclaim over the artwork Mei had created and to give Miriam the most cursory description of their long weekend.

Esther looked drawn, her eyes puffy, though she never dropped her smile, an effective defense against any serious conversation.

After they left, Miriam pulled the shades and lay down on the couch. Her shoulders and neck were tight with tension. She stared at the box of chocolates sitting on the coffee table, which Esther had given her in thanks for babysitting. Esther knew Miriam hadn't wanted to touch chocolate since her episode with the martinis.

Just a few days with Mei and she was completely tapped out. She was wholly unprepared for motherhood. She tried unsuccessfully not to cry.

It was hard to remember any former enthusiasm over having children. Paul had always been certain. He wanted to be a father, and tried to convince her that she would be a great mother. He charmed her with talk of Little League and camping, tea parties with stuffed animals, ballet recitals. All these scenarios he had spoken of with the same dreaminess with which she talked about romantic getaways on an exotic island.

Something shifted inside her, and she realized that she had never wanted children. She had not played with dolls growing up, had not dreamed of being a mother like some of her friends who had even claimed to look forward to the pain of childbirth. She had agreed to get pregnant because Paul had wanted it so much. She had done it only to please him.

With determination, she searched for the number of the woman's clinic. Her purse, the junk drawer, in the pile of paper by the phone. Her jeans. Yes, she vaguely recalled stuffing the doctor's note into her back pocket. She pawed through the pile of dirty clothes in her bedroom closet and found the note.

Standing beside the bed, she called before she lost her nerve, answering the person's questions mechanically, stunned that they could see her the following day. She was far enough along that they would have to do an ultrasound first and the procedure would probably require several trips to the clinic.

"Okay," she agreed, pushing the off button with her thumb. "Okay," she repeated to herself and crawled into bed.

# thirteen

*t*he clinic was tucked between drab office buildings with a surprisingly prominent sign that Miriam managed to miss

each time she circled the block, getting honked at once for changing lanes without checking her blind spot. She held the directions against the steering wheel, checking them frequently until, the third time around, finally, there it was. Still she passed it by, choosing instead to pull into a ramp several blocks away.

The car door echoed when she slammed it shut, and she was careful to note where she was so she wouldn't get lost on the way back. Her tennis shoes made no noise in the stairwell, but she could hear the clack made by someone's heels a few levels up.

As she stepped out of the relative shelter of the parking lot, the wind hit her with force, wrapping her hair around her face. She searched her pockets for an elastic band as she walked, but had to settle for holding her hair back with one hand. Her fingers ached with cold.

Standing at a busy corner, Miriam could see the clinic across the street and half a block away. The sound of a car horn startled her, and she expected to see a collision, but all the vehicles were evenly spaced and slowing for the yellow light. The car honked again, and she saw its driver lean across the passenger seat to wave to a group of people on the sidewalk who waved back and pumped their placards up and down.

Protesters. Three of them. In heavy winter jackets, stocking caps, and scarves over their chins, as if they didn't want their identities known any more than she did.

The light changed, and a man in a long wool coat stepped off the curb near Miriam and hurried across the street. She followed him. Her chest felt tight in the same way it had when as a teenager she walked home late at night after studying with a friend: Passing a house with thick hedges hugging the sidewalk, she'd force herself to keep a steady pace, knowing that if she looked over her shoulder or broke into a run, she was sunk.

This feeling pursued her to the front door of the clinic, where she stopped abruptly, unable to raise her hand to push open the door. If she were to step inside the waiting room, she imagined all the heads that would turn toward her, to note her entrance. The receptionist, a nurse, the others waiting; how many would there be? As she reached out to open the door, she realized that she couldn't bear the scrutiny of even one set of eyes.

She hurried back the way she had come, retracing her steps without lifting her gaze from the sidewalk. Her legs burned as she climbed the yeasty-smelling stairs, out of breath by the time she reached her car. She thought she had never heard such a welcome sound as the remote beep of the car unlocking, and she hunkered down in the front seat, turning the heat as high as it would go. She cupped her hands in the hot air blasting from the vents until they began to feel clammy.

The radio would be better than listening to her own thoughts. She snapped it on, cringing at the blast of country western and quickly pushing a different memory button. That, too, was programmed to the twang of country. She tried another, and another. All were tuned to the same station.

Paul had done this once before: programmed all her preset buttons to the same AM talk radio station, thinking he was so hilarious.

She took a deep, shuddery breath and listened to the Best of Country for a long time before heading home.


The grief support group met in a church she had passed every day on her way to work. The large A-frame building was sided with rough brown shingles, made drabber by the landscape beaten up by a winter of heavy snow and ice.

She pushed through the glass door and followed hastily penned signs to the basement. At the base of the stairs was a dehumidifier with frozen coils. Five round tables in the center of the large room were already filling with people, and a counter separating the main room from the kitchen sported two percolators and mounds of powdered-sugar donut holes. The musty odor of the basement, the boiled coffee smell, and the cheap bowls filled with non-dairy creamer reminded her of every church function she'd ever attended. Soothing, in a way. She filled out a name tag, poured a cup of coffee, then stood surveying the room, chewing the end of a stir stick.

A grandmotherly, white-haired woman caught her eye and patted an adjacent chair invitingly, so Miriam joined her.

"Joan," the woman pointed to her own name tag and shook Miriam's hand a little too long. "Your first time here?" she asked, squinting at Miriam's name.

"Is it that obvious?"

"It's a disadvantage to be the new person. Most of us have been coming for a while, so it's easy to spot the newbies. But don't be nervous. We were all new at one point."

"Thanks."

Miriam glanced at the man sitting directly across the table. Frank, his name tag declared in bold strokes. He was thin in his conservative blue suit and almost completely bald, though he looked to be in his early forties. He was staring at a single donut on the small napkin in front of him. He looked up and their eyes met. She wound the stir stick around her index finger, watching the tip turn blue.

A woman standing near the coffee pots asked for everyone's attention, and Miriam recognized her voice as the contact person she had spoken to on the phone. She introduced a speaker who planned to talk about the role of anger in the grieving process.

While the speaker got started, Miriam had a chance to observe the other people sitting at her table. Beside Frank was Janet, who wept silently, brushing tears away with the tips of her fingers, and next to her, Alex sat with his arms tightly crossed. He had a strong jaw, and Miriam could see a muscle working, as if he were clenching his teeth. He and Janet had the same last name.

And then there was Joan, whose perfume, Miriam now realized, was overpowering. Miriam blew on her coffee, sniffing the warm, creamy smell to calm her stomach.

While the speaker went through transparencies on "Owning Our Anger," Frank sat hunched over, glaring down at his donut hole as if he'd like to stab it. His dead wife, Ann, Miriam learned when they went around the table introducing themselves, had died of anorexia. The force of his anger scared him, he admitted.

"It's all very well and good to hear that I have a right to be angry at Ann because whatever I think or say can't hurt her. But my girls." He rubbed his hand over his face. "They're a different story."

Janet had stopped crying and now leaned forward, absently twisting a strand of her long, straight hair around an index finger, but clearly interested in what Frank was saying. She and her husband were there because their six-teen-year-old son had died of e-coli poisoning.

"Last Saturday I took Ashley and Erin to the mall," Frank continued, "to get them new Easter outfits. A nice, fatherly thing to do, right? They each tried on about three thousand outfits, which was enough to drive me mad, but the kicker for me was listening to them complain about how fat they are. Erin isn't petite like her sister or Ann was, but she's not fat. She stood in front of that stupid mirror and said how much she hates her butt and her upper arms and her neck, all those body parts that Ann obsessed about, even when she only weighed eighty-two pounds."

"How old is Erin?" Miriam asked.

"Ten."

"Sometimes girls complain about being fat not because they really believe they are, but because they want to hear someone tell them they're not," Janet offered.

"Honey," Alex said in a scathing voice. "Their mother was anorexic. I think it's a little more complicated than that."

Janet fiddled with the strap of her purse, which was on the table in front of her.

"I don't understand," Joan said. "Are you mad at your daughters or at your wife?"

Frank nodded. "Both. My kids. I was so mad, I wanted to shake them."

"Maybe they couldn't tell," Joan said.

"No, they knew. Ashley told Erin that she needed to start watching her calorie intake and I went ballistic. I told her that her mother had 'watched her calorie intake,' which led her straight to the morgue, and I didn't want to hear her say such a stupid thing ever again."

Miriam's whole body flushed with embarrassment for him, that he had said such a terrible thing to the girls about their own mother, and that he had admitted it in front of everyone. She could hardly imagine confessing this to Father Jake, let alone a bunch of strangers.

But without missing a beat, Alex said, "But you said it real compassionately, right? That part about the morgue."

Everyone, including Frank, laughed. "Yeah," he said. "Just like I told them very nicely and without any anger at all that they were going to have to wear rags to the Easter service this year because I'm not buying them new clothes anytime soon."

Eventually, talk moved to Alex and the litigation process he was involved in, suing the restaurant that had given their son e-coli.

When the meeting ended, Frank fell in step with Miriam on the way out of the building.

"I'm sorry about your girls," she said.

"I really blew it with them."

"Kids are resilient."

"Maybe. But I still blew it. Ashley still isn't speaking to me."

"Have you considered getting them into counseling?"

"I've broached the topic with them a few times, but they're resistant."

"Maybe you should make them go."

"My wife was in therapy," he said bitterly. "A fat lot of good it did her."

They had climbed the stairs and reached the front door. Miriam put her coat on, stepping aside so others could get out, nodding good-bye to those she had met.

She turned to face him. "I'm sorry. I shouldn't be offering advice," she apologized.

"It doesn't matter," he shrugged it off.

"Yes, it does. I've had so many people telling me what I should do lately that it makes me crazy. Why can't people just listen instead of giving advice? And here I am, doing the same thing to you. Just tell me to shut up."

Frank smiled. "No, actually, you're probably right. I feel like I battle them over so many things, I haven't wanted to introduce one more reason for them to hate me. But getting them into counseling is probably a battle worth fighting."

Miriam pulled her keys from her purse, trying not to jangle them too obviously.

Frank scuffed his shoe on the stained carpeting of the entryway. "Would you be interested in getting together for coffee sometime?"

Miriam was so stunned she didn't answer. She looked at him, then out at the parking lot, longingly.

"Or maybe you could come over on Friday night when the girls and I usually rent a movie. Have popcorn. That sort of thing."

"I'm—" she stopped to clear her throat. "I've only been a widow about three months."

"It wouldn't have to be a date," he said desperately. "I'm not ready for that, either. I'd like you to meet Ashley and Erin. I think you'd like them. And they could use a good, female role model."

Miriam started to protest that he didn't know her well enough to presume she'd be a good role model, but swallowed her words at the naked look on his face. She could see how clearly he wanted her to say yes. She dug in her purse for a piece of paper and scribbled her number on it.

His happiness as he shoved it in his pocket was palpable. "I'll call you," he said as they headed toward their cars, and she had no doubt he would.

Trying not to be angry at herself for being such a fool, she thought that perhaps she could be of some help to his girls. Things must truly be terrible for them right now.

At home, Miriam flipped through a few photo albums, searching for her favorite picture, one of the few that had both her and Paul in it. She felt that she had given Frank a piece of herself when she identified herself as a widow; it was the first time she had vocalized this. She wanted to stop thinking about Frank and his girls. It scared her that even when she concentrated hard, Paul's image in her mind was growing indistinct, like seeing a person at a distance through a downpour.

She found the picture she was looking for, slipped it from its slot, and took it upstairs with her, perching on the edge of the tub as it filled.

Sliding down into the warmth, she held the picture carefully above the water. It was the day of his graduation from law school. He was in his cap and gown and had his arm thrown around her neck, pulling her close. She was in profile, kissing his cheek, but it was obvious she was smiling. They both looked so happy. Bursting. He had proposed later that night.

"I should have told Frank I'm pregnant," she told the two-dimensional Paul. "I'm sorry."

She cried from deep within her body, letting the photo drop into the bath water, where it floated in lazy circles above her belly.

*b*ecause the hospital had called to confirm her appointment for an ultrasound, and because she didn't want to have to explain to Henry why she had missed it, Miriam reluctantly showed up. She waited in the room by herself a long time, trying not to think about how much she needed to go to the bathroom, having been told to drink plenty of fluids so she'd have a full bladder for the exam.

When the ultrasound technician finally showed up, she didn't greet Miriam or look at her where she lay on the table before shifting the gown to expose Miriam's belly, unapologetically squeezing on a glob of cold jelly and fiddling with the settings on the machine.

Miriam stared at the ceiling with as much concentration as if she were in a dentist's chair. The tech wielded the ultrasound wand with a lot of force, digging deep into Miriam's side. She wondered if she had done something to offend the woman or if she considered all patients to be intrusions. The sound of a steady heartbeat filled the room.

"Could you turn that off?" Miriam asked, still looking at the ceiling.

"The machine?"

"The sound. Please. I don't want to hear it."

The technician puffed out her cheeks in annoyance, but did as Miriam asked. Soon Miriam's entire belly was smeared with jelly and had been roughly probed.

"It's a boy," the tech declared without asking if Miriam wanted this information. "Your doctor will call you if anything is wrong."

"Thank you," Miriam said, grateful that if nothing else, the exam was over.

"You didn't look at the screen, so maybe you'd like this," the tech said, dropping a picture on Miriam's chest and pushing away from the table. "You can leave as soon as you're ready." She stopped with a hand on the door, asked: "This is your first pregnancy?"

"Yes."

"Ah," she said, as though that explained everything.

On Good Friday, Miriam visited the cemetery for the first time since the burial. The headstone would be in place by now, she knew, though she couldn't remember what it looked like, what she had chosen.

Once inside the pillared gate, she found the road branched and twisted like a haphazard maze. She remembered seeing the blocky mausoleum on the right, remembered how cold the angel with unfurled wings looked on top of that grave. The cemetery felt open but crowded at the same time, with very few trees breaking up the space between the simple grave markers that lay flat against the ground and the wildly ornate ones that reached for the sky.

Leaving the car, Miriam wandered past the graves, noting how many headstones had ending dates for the men and only birth dates for their wives. Brown grass crunched underfoot, but there was a softness to the ground that meant spring was on its way.

Miriam stopped in front of a grave with plastic, yellow tulips thrust randomly into the ground. Mr. Cooper had died eight years previously, and apparently Mrs. Cooper was still going strong. Miriam wondered how long they had been married. Eight years was a long time to be apart, longer than the length of her marriage. Someone had told her after the funeral that it took half the number of years of a marriage to get over a death or a divorce—as if it were a blessing that they hadn't been married longer.

An old woman in hip waders obviously made for a much larger person was kneeling next to a site, working the ground with a trowel. She lifted her arm and thrust the metal point into the earth, making a rhythmic chinking noise that crossed the cemetery like a gunshot. In the distance a small dog yipped, and beyond that was the drone of traffic.

There it was. The blue granite headstone, ground to a slippery finish on the front, KOVATCH etched along the top. No Scripture to offend Henry, no cute saying to offend Paul. Just Paul Andrew on the bottom left with his dates, and her name on the right, with only one date, emptiness after the dash.

"What if you remarry?" Theresa had asked, staring at her pointedly in the silence that followed. "What'll you do then?"

She wished she could be angry at Theresa, but even now, she couldn't summon the energy for it.

Someone had left an Easter lily on the ground under Paul's name. The white flowers bobbed in the slight breeze above the pot wrapped in pink cellophane and tied with a yellow bow. Miriam had brought nothing to decorate the grave.

She didn't stay long, but soon trudged back to her car, hands plunged deep in her pockets, grateful that someone else was out there, missing Paul, too.


The Good Friday service had started by the time she settled into a side pew, keeping her head down as if that would prevent Father Jake from noticing her. The thought of being seen by him was almost as terrifying as talking to him, even for confession. Yet she hadn't wanted to miss the service. Skipping weekly mass was one thing. Skipping Good Friday and Easter was another.

The solemnity of the service suited her. Father was dressed in a robe the color of blood, and the chancel, altar, and crucifix were draped in black. Christ was a man of sorrows and acquainted with grief, the priest reminded her.

As the service came to a close, the lights slowly dimmed while Father Jake proceeded out of the sanctuary, taking with him the last flickering candle. Plunged into nearly absolute darkness, Miriam felt a flutter deep inside, a butterfly flitting against the confines of skin and muscle. Undeniable, what that sensation was. She had felt intimations of this before, but had been uncertain, thinking perhaps it was gas or indigestion or imagination. Now, however, she had in mind fingers and toes and quick swimming strokes: a delicate presence that she had chosen to create for the wrong reason and had chosen to keep out of fear. How could you want something and not want it at the same time?

Pulling herself off the hard pew, she slipped out a side door the moment the lights came back on.

Suzi called, ecstatic that she had managed to schedule a full day of showings. Two couples in the morning, a family in the afternoon, surely a MOTIVATED buyer in there somewhere. "Now, all we need to do is find a new home for YOU!"

Perhaps inspired, or else responding to the mounting pressure, Miriam suggested she would like to look at houses in Steven's neighborhood. It was an older area with wide streets, mature trees, modest architecture. As she spoke, she realized that she actually could picture herself there.

Suzi warned her that homes didn't often go for sale in that area, but without losing any enthusiasm. "I'm sure we'll find SOMEthing," she said, brightly.

On the day of the showings, Miriam had to vacate the house for the day. Tired of wearing jogging pants with elastic waistbands that left puckered fabric marks on her skin, Miriam headed to the mall. Later that evening she was going to Steven's for a dinner party, where she'd be meeting Joseph.

Another good reason to buy some new clothes, she thought, as she pulled a maternity dress over her head and settled it around her body.

Why designers put bows on maternity clothes was beyond her. She plucked at the pink bow resting on top of her belly, frowning at her image in the mirror. As if being pregnant was supposed to make her want to dress like a three-year-old. She looked like a frumpy, beached whale.

She pulled off the dress and took a good look at her nearly naked body. Her thighs had grown along with her stomach, and a few narrow stripes of pink emerged from the top of her panties and reached for her belly button. Stretch marks. *Lovely.* The blood vessels were more prominent beneath the skin of her breasts, and she undid her bra for a closer look. Her normally light areolas had turned dark brown. She settled back into the bra, wondering what Paul would think of all this. She couldn't imagine him finding her ungainly body attractive. And it was only going to get worse.

She stepped into a denim skirt with the requisite stretchy front panel and chose a green blouse to go with it. The skirt, she had to admit, cradled her stomach just right, and the blouse, devoid of fussy bows or painted buttons, wasn't too bad. The relief at getting out of her ill-fitting, constricting clothes was strong. How many days had she sat in front of the television with her jeans unzipped or the elastic pushed below the mound of her belly, stupidly refusing to go shopping?

She knew why, though. The cut and style of maternity clothes made it readily apparent that she was pregnant. She could no longer hide beneath Paul's baggy sweatshirts, pretending before the world that the weight gain was simply a widow drowning her very understandable grief in chocolate and cookies.

A salesperson helped her cut the tags off a pair of black pants and a crisp, pleated white shirt so she could wear them out of the store.

"You look beautiful," the woman said, placing her hands on Miriam's sides and smoothing the fabric of her blouse. "Look at that. You've still got your waist. When I was pregnant, I grew sideways instead of forward."

Miriam looked over her shoulder at the three-way mirror. "All I see is a big butt," she said.

The woman laughed. "Most pregnant women feel that way." She helped gather the piles of clothes Miriam had chosen and led the way to a cash register. "I guess we have to listen to our husbands when they tell us how gorgeous we are and try to make ourselves believe that they're telling the truth. After all, theirs is the only opinion that matters, right?"

Miriam was embarrassed by how quickly her eyes filled with tears.

The saleswoman looked alarmed. "Did I say something wrong? I'm sorry. I didn't mean anything bad—"

"No," Miriam lied, digging in her purse for a credit card to speed up the transaction. "Just hormones."

She had a few more hours before she needed to be at Steven's to help him get ready for the party, so she stopped by the library and wandered the stacks, gravitating toward her favorite books. In her previous life, on days when she felt listless or in need of inspiration, she could always peruse magazines of the latest architectural trends or books filled with stunning images: *Architecture of the Poor, Buildings that Changed the World, The Not So Big House.* But nothing was able to hold her attention.

She stepped into the darkened microfiche room, just to look around, and a librarian seated at a desk near the door asked if she needed any help. Without thinking, Miriam requested a *Tribune* from the year she was in second grade. She had never before had any desire to research the fire at her parochial school. It might be interesting to read the newspaper accounts, to get an adult perspective.

The librarian returned with a box of film and found Miriam where she waited at an unoccupied machine. Over Miriam's shoulder, the woman threaded the film between two glass plates, adjusted the microscope, and wound the free end of the film around an empty cartridge. She demonstrated how to adjust the focus and zip from one section of the newspaper to another. The projected newsprint blurred on the screen, pictures flashing past so quickly they were headache-inducing. The woman released the lever, bringing the machine to an abrupt halt between two pages, and patted Miriam on the back before heading back to her desk.

The room was crowded with oversized file cabinets full of newspapers that had been transferred to film. People sat elbow to elbow at their individual machines, ghosts of light and shadow flickering across their faces. They all looked equally intent, and Miriam wondered what they were searching for. Two elderly women leaned toward each other in their chairs, whispering.

Miriam turned back to her screen and scrolled the newspaper slowly forward. When she reached the date of the fire, the headline leapt out. "School Fire, 90 DEAD"

*Holy Mother of God.*

She had forgotten how many died. Or perhaps she had never known. The school had been destroyed, so after several surgeries and months of recuperation and physical therapy, she had been sent to a new school, where she was cognizant only of Vinny's absence.

In the middle of the page was a panoramic view of the school on fire, and below that, a photo of adults crowding the sidewalk with furrowed brows and stricken looks on their faces. Miniature school portraits lined the bottom of the article, putting faces to some of the victims' names.

One little girl with tight braids that dangled below her chin was a classmate whose desk had been closest to the door. All the faces looked familiar, even those who were in Vinny's grade or higher. She looked at each young face tentatively, relieved that her brother's picture was not shown among them.

She went back to the beginning and read.

Misery etches the faces of parents as they wait for word of missing children. Shouts of joy and cries of despair ring out in hospital lounges and on the streets outside the school. . . .

Nuns and firemen stumble out of the building, soot blacker than night obscuring their features. The thick smoke from the fire which originated in the stairwell overwhelmed classroom after classroom before anyone could sound the alarm.

Vinny's classroom was at the corner of the building, right next to the stairwell, so it would have been the first to succumb to smoke. Only a few of his classmates survived; the fatalities were highest in the rooms closest to the stairs. About half of Miriam's class survived.

A friend of Miriam's mother had told her that she was special because God had saved her from the fire. "Be thankful," the woman had said in the confident, commanding tone with which well-meaning adults address children when they have a moral to impart. Miriam had nodded obediently, tucking the words beneath a protest she was too young to express. Vinny had been special, too, so where did that leave her?

The article went on for ten pages. She scrolled forward and stopped when a name caught her eye.

Edwin Deluca was supposed to wait—

Miriam made a small noise and snatched her hands to her chest. The man sitting to her left didn't look her way, which she hoped meant he hadn't heard her. She tried to breathe normally. Deluca was her maiden name. Edwin, her father.

Edwin Deluca was supposed to wait with the other parents in the lounge, but somehow managed to get by guards and into the sanctuary of the nearby church which had been turned into an emergency room for some thirty young fire victims.

Patiently, he went from cot to cot, asking the small occupants: "Have you seen my Vinny? Where is my Miriam?" But they could not tell him the fate of his nine-year-old son or seven-year-old daughter.

A bead of sweat threaded its way down the nape of Miriam's neck and between her shoulder blades. She realized she was tugging at her necklace and forced herself to stop.

Her father wasn't mentioned again, though she searched several days' worth of newspapers, hoping for a follow-up. She wanted to know if he continued his search for her even after he identified Vinny's charred body. Or did, as she feared, the sight so confound him that he gave up? Did he, perhaps, peek into the hospital room where she lay bandaged and pinned together, glad that she, at least, was alive?

No matter how much she wished it otherwise, as far as she could recall, her father never again uttered either her or Vinny's name aloud, effectively rendering her as invisible as her brother was dead.

Miriam rewound the microfiche with trembling fingers and returned it to the librarian.

She drove to Steven's with careful deliberation.

## fifteen

"Steven, where are the twirly things that go with your mixer?" In the process of making chocolate éclairs for Steven's dinner party, Miriam was searching through his utensil drawer fruitlessly.

"'Twirly things?'"

"I can't think of what they're called, Mister Smarty-Pants."

"Attachments, darling. In there," he pointed with his knife before turning back to the onion he was chopping.

"I swear my brain is turning to mush the bigger the baby gets. The other day I got lost coming home from the grocery store, where I've only been a million times." She dug through a jumble of wooden spoons and spatulas.

"Could you tell me where else you might have hidden *the attachments?* There's only one dough hook and one regular kind in here."

"That's it."

"What do you mean, that's it?"

"I mean you have to use the mismatched pair. It's all I've got."

"How on earth does a person lose one of each?"

"Brian took them when he left."

Miriam clapped a hand over her mouth. "I'm sorry. I shouldn't laugh."

"Let's see. He also took all my flat sheets, leaving the fitted, all my right shoes, and every single light bulb." He put the chopped onion in a pan to sauté them. "Actually," he corrected, "he didn't take the bulbs. He threw them down the basement stairs."

"Steven, you have got to improve your taste in men."

"I admit it. I was young and stupid."

"You've gotten smarter recently?"

"Wait until you meet Joseph."

"Does that mean you'll listen if I tell you he's not right for you?"

"Absolutely."

"You are such a liar," Miriam laughed.

She took the pan of boiling water and butter off the stove, mixed in the flour with a spoon, broke an egg, and started the mixer. Batter exploded up and out, splattering the wall and cupboards and the front of Miriam's white blouse with greasy droplets. "Steven!" she wailed.

"It's not my fault," he protested, tossing her a towel.

She dabbed at her shirt, hoping the wet spots would dry before Joseph arrived.

"Brian was six years ago, right? And in all that time you never thought to buy a new mixer?"

Smirking, he handed her a whisk.

The fresh rosemary and lemon stuffing that Steven was mixing with his fingers smelled wonderful. Her nausea, which had stubbornly persisted into her sixth month of pregnancy, had calmed, but out of sheer inertia she was still subsisting on cereal, mashed potatoes, and plain toast, with vegetables thrown in once in a while to keep her doctor's scolding to a minimum. Relaxing into the rhythm of cooking with Steven, bantering and sneaking a mouthful of stuffing when he wasn't looking, Miriam could almost believe she was human again.

The guests all arrived at once, perfectly timed. The long wooden table was beautifully set with fresh flowers, white linens, and Steven's pottery dishes, the smell of roast chicken and sautéed vegetables warming the air.

Miriam stood, speechless, as Esther, Charles, Jenny, her husband Kevin, and Ben and a young woman she didn't know crowded into the entryway. They were all carrying gifts and, understanding, Miriam called to Steven, "You had me make my own birthday dessert?!"

Charles slung an arm around her neck and kissed her cheek as Steven spread his hands in a don't-blame-me gesture. His smile was big, but his eyes pleaded with her to have a nice time, for his surprise to be a good one.

"Here he is," Steven exclaimed, pointing beyond her through the still-open front door.

Miriam swung around, hope flaring crazily in her stomach as she half-expected to see Paul running up the sidewalk, freshly showered from a basketball game at the Y, gift in hand, late as usual.

But it was a man she had never seen before.

"My very good friend and poet, Joseph," Steven introduced.

Miriam shook his hand, smiling gamely and wanting to punch herself for being so stupid.

Steven moved everyone into the living room, where Miriam greeted Jenny, who was hugely pregnant.

"Can you believe it?" her friend said, shyly, both hands caressing her stomach.

"Wonderful," Miriam nodded.

"I wanted to tell you before, but it just didn't . . ." she paused awkwardly. "But look at *you!* How long were you going to keep your news a secret?"

"Oh, I don't know. Until the kid turned eighteen?"

Jenny laughed. "We'll have to have a baby shower for you. Is your sister planning one?"

She could think of very few things she wanted less. "Not that I know of. But that's okay, I don't really want one."

"What are you talking about? You have to have a shower for your first baby!"

"To be honest, I don't know if I could handle it," Miriam admitted desperately. "I'm having enough trouble coming to terms with the pregnancy; I can't imagine having a party to focus on it."

Jenny looked concerned. "But aren't you excited about having a baby? I was thinking you'd be glad to have something to remind you of Paul."

Kevin, who had been talking to Steven, joined them, relieving her of the necessity to respond. "Look at you two, so beautiful and pregnant." He kissed Miriam gently on the cheek before insisting on taking their picture.

Despite her protests, he posed them standing sideways to emphasize their profiles, and through her smile, Miriam realized she was officially in hell.

"Perfect," Kevin announced before turning to take someone else's picture.

Ben was waiting to introduce her to his friend Tina. Miriam was in no doubt about their relationship when Ben put his arm around the young woman, tucking her against his side. She was a petite thing with a delicate nose and mouth, and long blonde hair fashionably highlighted with dark chocolate streaks.

"If you talk to my Mom," Ben said, "don't tell her you saw us. She doesn't know we're here."

Miriam made a zipping motion over her mouth. "Have you met Ben's parents yet?"

"Not yet," Tina said. "We're meeting them on Sunday for lunch before we head back to school."

"They think we're coming up for the day," Ben explained.

"I'm sure they'll love you."

"They'd better," Ben said with the easy confidence of new love.

"Do you guys need a place to stay until Sunday?"

"Uncle Steven is letting us stay here. It's weird, but Mom doesn't freak out over him anymore. She could hardly stand to hear his name before and now she's inviting him over for dinner and doesn't care when I see him."

They all looked through the doorway into the kitchen, where Steven and Esther were chatting.

"It's the one good thing to come out of all of this," Ben continued. "Besides the baby, of course."

Confused at first, and as though her mind were flooded with glue, Miriam had to work to process this statement. It was an utterly foreign and unwelcome thought, that anything good could come of Paul's death.

"What?" she asked, suddenly aware that Ben had asked her something.

"Have you decorated the nursery yet? Tina and I were thinking we could come over tomorrow and help you paint if you want."

"Oh," she said in surprise. "No, I'm probably going to move before the baby comes, so I won't set up a nursery until then."

"Have you found a new place?"

"Not yet. I haven't told Steven yet, but I'm looking for a place in this neighborhood. If it works out, I'll surprise him."

"Well, when you move, let me know. I can carry boxes. And furniture." He flexed the arm that wasn't around Tina. "I've been working out."

Tina giggled.

Miriam left them discussing political science professors with Charles, who was thrilled to find out they were attending his alma mater. She found Esther and Steven still in the kitchen, opening bottles of wine.

"How're you doing?" Esther asked, nudging Miriam's shoulder.

"I was going to ask you the same thing."

"If Kevin refers to Jenny as his 'beautiful pregnant wife' one more time, I may have to kill him," Esther said.

Miriam gave her an understanding squeeze and accepted a glass of sparkling grape juice from Steven. "Does Joseph have wine yet?" she asked.

Steven shook his head and Miriam offered to take him a glass. "I haven't had a chance to talk to him. Esther, keep my brother occupied while I'm gone."

"Oh, great," Steven groaned. "This can't be good."

Joseph was in the living room, leaning against the fireplace mantel, which was crowded with photos. She noted with some irritation that he was handsome. Tall, fit, chiseled jaw, lively green eyes, deliberately mussed silver hair. He wore jeans and a black t-shirt. Looked like a poet. And a heartbreaker.

"Obscene, isn't it?" she said, handing him the glass.

"What is?"

"All those pictures of me."

He laughed. "I can see why Steven's crazy about you," he pointed to a picture of a young Miriam sitting on a park swing, her sandaled-feet dangling. "It was a bit strange, all these pictures of a beautiful brunette. You two don't look like each other the way some siblings do."

"There are so many years between us, it's no wonder we look a lot different."

Joseph pointed to another photo. "That's Jeremy, right?"

"Yes," Steven answered from behind Miriam. "He died ten years ago."

Miriam was surprised Joseph didn't know this already. He and Steven had been seeing each other for long enough she assumed they would have covered their past histories in depth. Steven was watching Joseph, a nakedly affectionate look on his face.

"AIDS?" Joseph asked.

"Cancer."

Joseph's respectful nod and silence impressed Miriam. She'd heard other gay men say, "lucky him," as though nothing, even agonizing stomach cancer, could be as bad as dying of AIDS.

Maybe Steven would be okay with Joseph, after all.

During dinner, Jenny turned the conversation to pregnancy again. "When's your due date?" she wanted to know.

"August."

"August what?"

"I don't remember exactly," Miriam said, glancing across the table to where Esther was cutting her green beans with great concentration.

"How could you forget the date? We've been counting down the days ever since we found out what ours is. June third."

Miriam tried to think of a way to change the subject for Esther's sake without making Jenny feel bad.

"Have you signed up for Lamaze?" Jenny persisted.

Miriam shook her head.

"You should do that soon. The classes fill up fast. I'll give you the name of our instructor. She's so nice. Even Kevin thinks the classes are a ton of fun, don't you, honey?"

"Those classes don't really help all that much," Esther said. "Once labor hits you, all that breathe-deep crap goes right out the window. It's pure instinct from then on. Believe me. You'll be begging for an epidural."

"All right," Charles laughed, placing a hand on Esther's arm. "We're in mixed company. Let's scare the pregnant ladies later."

Everyone laughed.

"So, Joseph," Miriam said nervously in the silence that followed, "how long have you been writing poetry?"

After dessert and coffee, Miriam opened her presents. A bottle of lotion and fragrant soaps, a certificate to a spa, a set of deep-purple flannel sheets. Ben gave her colored pencils and drafting paper, a gift so thoughtful it choked her up. Then Charles asked Joseph to help him carry something in from his car.

They toted in a large, rectangular box wrapped in brown paper and decorated with magic marker balloons and birthday cakes, which she recognized as Mei's handiwork. With Charles holding the gift steady, Miriam pulled off the paper, careful to save a few of Mei's drawings to put on her refrigerator.

"Is it really?" she wondered aloud, and Charles nodded. A drafting table. Beautiful, wooden, smooth design.

Exactly what she would have chosen herself, only more expensive.

"How on earth . . ." She looked around the room in disbelief. What would possess her friends to get her such a thing? She knelt on the floor to get a closer look at the picture on the box. The table was solid oak with six locking drawers down the right side, a storage cabinet in back, and a white melamine top with an adjustable angle.

"It's perfect," she said, thinking it must have cost a fortune. "Did you all go in on this together?"

Charles and Esther exchanged a look.

"It's from Paul," Esther said quietly. "He wanted to surprise you, so he had it shipped to our place. It was supposed to be a Christmas present."

The room was absolutely silent except for the soft sound of jazz from the stereo.

"Oh my God, Esther," Jenny said in an accusing tone.

Steven helped Miriam get up from her kneeling position.

She turned away from the gift, acutely aware of everyone's eyes on her. "Excuse me," she said. "I think I need to use the bathroom."

She climbed the stairs and slipped into Steven's room. If she waited long enough, maybe everyone would just leave. Or maybe she'd wake up and find this was all a bad dream.

Esther found her there, sitting in an armchair. "You okay?" she asked, handing over a box of tissue from Steven's dresser.

"Esther, I can't believe you did that to me."

Esther seemed surprised by this. "I'm sorry. I guess we didn't really think about how you'd feel."

Miriam felt a flash of anger. "No, you didn't. You blindsided me in front of everyone. Why on earth didn't you give it to me at Christmas, or at the very least, in private?"

"It didn't arrive until after the funeral. And then there was so much else going on, I kept forgetting about it."

"You forgot about it? And when you remembered, you decided it would be a good idea to wrap it for my birthday? That's—" she searched for a word that eluded her. "Unbelievable," was all she could come up with.

"I didn't know it would hurt you like this." Esther sat on the edge of the bed, refusing to look at Miriam. "I don't know what you want me to say."

Miriam rubbed her eyes, feeling bone-weary. She heard voices downstairs and the front door opening and closing. "I don't understand what's been going on between us lately. Are you punishing me for something? It's only been five months since Paul died, which might seem like a long time, but it's not. If I'm bringing you down, I wish you'd just tell me so I could leave you alone."

"No, it's not that."

"Then what is it?"

"There's stuff going on in my life, too, you know. But you've been so wrapped up in your own pain that I haven't been able to tell you."

"Like about your miscarriage?"

"How did you know?" Esther asked, more angry than surprised.

"Mei told me."

"Yeah, my miscarriage," Esther confirmed, beginning to cry. "I was fifteen weeks along."

"Why didn't you tell me?"

"I tried. Believe me."

"You did?" Baffled, Miriam felt her anger rising again. "When? And I didn't listen?"

"It's just so unfair I can hardly stand to—" Esther seemed to catch herself and grabbed a tissue.

As Estheer glanced toward Miriam and then quickly away, Miriam understood her unfinished sentence to be: *I can hardly stand to be with you.*

"It's not just the unfairness of the miscarriages and the fact that every crack-head prostitute can carry a baby to term when I can't, it's—" She stood up and dug in a pocket, pulling out an elastic band that she used to twist her hair into a ponytail. Miriam recognized the angry gesture. "I just can't stand that you're pregnant and I'm not, okay? It's like a sick joke or something."

Miriam was stunned. "But I would give anything for you to be pregnant instead of me. How could you not know that?"

"I mean, what is God *thinking?* It's like, 'Let's find a way to rub Esther's nose in it. Oh, I know, let's get Miriam—who doesn't even want kids—pregnant!'" Esther blew her nose and leaned into the bureau mirror to check her mascara before turning toward the door.

Miriam stared at her back.

"Never mind," Esther said. "I'll get over it."

"Esther," Miriam protested, but her friend had already gone downstairs and was urging Charles out the door.

In Steven's bathroom, Miriam knelt in front of the toilet and waited, but nothing happened. Her stomach felt like a stone beneath her fingertips. She stayed in that position until her legs began to tingle and heartburn flared beneath her ribs. Pulling herself to her feet, she opened Steven's medicine cabinet, looking for Tums, and instead found bottle after bottle of prescription drugs—pills to be taken two, three, four times a day. She didn't recognize the scientific names, but she could guess their purpose.

A knock on the door made her jump and she shut the cabinet, wincing when it banged loudly.

"Miriam?" Steven called. "You okay in there?"

She opened the door.

"Darling." Steven touched her cheek with his fingertips and she pulled away. "If they told me what they were going to do, I would've prevented it. It was an incredibly stupid thing to do."

"Have you tried to tell me?"

He furrowed his eyebrows in confusion. "About the drafting table? I didn't know about it."

"Have I shut you out? Been too selfish about my own loss to listen to what's going on in your life?"

Steven searched her face. "Is that what Esther said?"

Without moving her eyes from his, Miriam swung open the medicine cabinet, revealing its careful rows of drugs. He looked at the bottles as if seeing them for the first time, then back at her. Reaching out, he shut the cabinet and pulled her from the bathroom, closing the door behind him.

"I didn't want you to worry about me."

Miriam bristled. "Don't patronize me. I'm not nine years old anymore." She crossed her arms and planted herself in front of him. "Why didn't you tell me?"

"You don't need any extra burdens. Plus, it's not like being HIV positive is the death sentence it used to be. A person can have it for years without being sick."

"How long have you had it?"

"Six years."

"Does Joseph know?"

Steven looked away from her, rubbed his hands across his face. "Yes," he answered, quietly.

She surprised herself by wanting to slap him. "You tell your brand new boyfriend, who could be a serial killer for all you know, but you don't get around to telling me in six years?"

"I'm sorry, Miriam."

A noise at the door yanked their attention from one another.

"Dude," said Ben, poking his head around the corner. "What's going on?"

"Ask your Uncle Steven," Miriam spat out, pushing past him. "Not that he'll tell you."

"Aunt Miriam!" Ben called after her, and she heard Steven's voice telling him to let her go.

## sixteen

*M*iriam shoved the suitcase into the trunk with such force the car bounced up and down. She had already given up trying to get the kayak on top. After a sleepless night, she had gotten up, determined to drive north, away from Chicago and the drone of traffic, the scrutiny of friends and family, the smog that made it difficult to breathe. Perhaps to follow through on her and Paul's plans to go camping in Wisconsin's Door County. Minus the kayak, she didn't know what she'd do.

She had witnessed Paul securing the kayak a thousand times, but what took him a heft of the arm or a turn of the wrist was impossible for her. Bruises were already knotting up along her legs from the times the boat tumbled down as she tried to hoist it over her head. She unstrapped the rack from the roof of the car and kicked it viciously.

Figment, stuck in his animal carrier, was meowing plaintively from the back seat of the car. A bag of kitty litter and an old cake pan were already wedged beside the suitcase.

She was standing by the open trunk when an unfamiliar car pulled into the driveway. Fear that it was Steven or Esther was followed quickly by irritation that she had opened the garage door and so could not avoid whoever it was. She shielded her eyes against the sun's glare, her other hand on her hip. Impatient.

A woman got out of the car and closed the door with a swift kick, then leaned heavily against it as though she knew it wouldn't stay closed without persuasion. The car was an old Geo Metro, tinny and full of rust, the front bumper held in place with duct tape.

Miriam recognized her. "Svetlana."

"Hello," she said, the "h" vibrating in the back of her throat. "I'm sorry to drop by, but it's my day off. I wanted to find out how are you."

"Why?" A rude question, but now that it was out, Miriam couldn't think of a way to soften it.

"I think of Mr. Kovatch often. Every day I think of you, too, and wish I could help somehow. The only thing I can think of is that I am a master cleaner. Your tub will shine like a mirror when I am through with it. I think maybe you need my help especially now," she observed, gesturing meaningfully toward Miriam's stomach. "It's no good for you to bend over or breathe fumes. Bad for the baby."

Miriam frowned. Why would this woman want to clean her bathtub? "I don't understand."

"Look at this letter I want to show you. See," she unfolded a piece of paper that was deeply creased from being read and re-read. "My husband was deported." She laughed a deep, throaty laugh, as though it were a grand joke. "He should be buried deep in the ground, but sent back to Russia? Is next best thing."

Miriam took the official-looking letter, feeling she should say something but unable to get beyond the confusion of what this had to do with her. Svetlana was watching her with a look of happy expectation.

"Your husband," Svetlana said. "He did this."

"Did what?"

"He talked many times with INS about my husband, explaining that he is not good citizen for United States. The lawyer I have now, he is not so good as your husband because he doesn't really understand." She accepted the letter back from Miriam and folded it carefully. "So this good result is all because of Mr. Kovatch. I can't thank him, so I thank you instead."

Picking up the second suitcase, Miriam tried to make it fit on top of the first.

"Here. Let me." Svetlana took the suitcase and gently nudged it into place. "You are going somewhere?"

Miriam put the cat carrier into the back seat and slammed the door. "Yes."

"Where?"

"I don't know."

"You are going on vacation?"

"No." Miriam pressed a hand to her forehead to ward off a headache. "I just need to get away."

"You will visit friends, perhaps?"

She thought of Esther, shrouded in anger. "No. I just—" she dropped her hand to her side in frustration.

Svetlana closed the trunk and waited.

"I just need to get away," she repeated. "I don't know where."

Svetlana squinted into the sun, then looked back at Miriam. "I understand," she said, quietly, and somehow Miriam believed that she did. "Are you ready to go? Everything is packed?"

"Yes."

"The house, it is locked?"

"Not yet."

"Okay, I am waiting here."

Miriam walked through the house to see if she had forgotten anything, and checked all the doors to make sure they were locked. She wondered if, when she went back to the garage, Svetlana would still be waiting or if there would merely be the shimmer of a mirage above the driveway.

But she was still there, resting her large frame against the back of the car, lifting her face into the warm sunshine.

"Ready?" she asked, and Miriam nodded. "Okay, you follow me."

The command didn't surprise or antagonize Miriam. Instead she felt strangely relieved to have someone else stepping in and making a decision, relieved to be allowed to just follow. Unresisting, she got in her car and drove on faith that the Russian woman knew what she was doing.

Figment began yowling at an octave unnatural and disconcerting the moment she backed out of the driveway. If she weren't following someone in a beat-up, smoking car, Miriam would have driven much faster, propelled by an impulse to get away from the unlikely sounds emanating from a four-pound kitten.

She turned the radio on, still set to a country station, pushing the volume loud and louder, stunning the cat into brief silence. But she couldn't stand the volume herself and turned it off. A semi passed on the left, battering the car with a gusty roar.

Figment yowled again, a long wavering note of discontent, and Miriam knew if they didn't get there—wherever *there* was—soon, she'd lose her mind. She called his name in her most soothing tone, reaching dangerously into the back seat to twiddle her fingers between the front grate of the carrier, reminding him that she was right there, that the car's noise was harmless. As if a cat could be reasoned out of terror.

Finally, Svetlana took a long, curving exit, and Miriam stuck close behind, feeling her body press against the door. The carrier slid across the back seat, and Figment's lunatic cry turned frantic.

The ramp dumped them at the edge of a concrete and asphalt wasteland. EZ-ON EZ-OFF, hollered a billboard above a gas station. Neon lights pointed to drive-thru windows of every fast food imaginable, and hotels enticed with claims of free wireless access and indoor water parks: Moosewood Lodge, WaterFun Resort, Silver Eight Motel where "Kids Eat Free."

Overwhelmed by the display of so many options, Miriam gratefully pulled into a parking spot next to Svetlana at the Moosewood Lodge, where a Bunyan-sized moose towered improbably over the building. Shadows played on the wall of the hotel as the sun, hindered by clouds, flickered through the moose's antlers.

Figment fell silent when she turned off the ignition, his breathing audible, like a dog panting. She leaned her head back and closed her eyes, thinking she could fall asleep in this position, until Svetlana tapped on the window.

Stepping into the lobby, it became clear that Svetlana knew the man working behind the desk.

"What are you doing here?" he asked her. "Isn't it your day off?"

"I love it so much here, I couldn't even stay away," Svetlana joked. "No, not really. My friend needs a room on the first floor. The elevator, you know, makes her feel sick."

Miriam wondered at this, but kept quiet when Svetlana winked at her, rallying herself only enough to answer the man's questions. When asked how long she would be staying, she said, "Forever," not joining in his laughter and amending her answer with a shrug. "A week. I guess."

With a plastic band clipped to her wrist for entry into the water park, Miriam drove around to the back of the building where Svetlana helped smuggle Figment through the sliding glass door directly into the room.

"Cats are not allowed," Svetlana shrugged implacably. "We get around that, no problem."

Svetlana shut the curtains, throwing the room into dusk, and poured some cat food into a dish for Figment. The air-conditioning unit, turned to low, created a nice hum of white noise. Numbly, Miriam watched all this from the edge of the bed. When Svetlana began helping her out of her clothes, she offered no resistance and felt no embarrassment in being so unveiled. Through the warmth of the woman's touch, Miriam sensed no questions or judgment, no shock over the reality of a body in its twenty-fourth week of pregnancy.

Svetlana threw back the covers of the bed so she could crawl between the sheets in her bra and panties, then helped settle pillows at her back and between her knees.

"I will come back tomorrow and look for you," Svetlana whispered, and to Miriam her words sounded like an answer to prayer. "Your secret," she said. "It is safe here, in this place, and with me."

Miriam wondered what secret that was. The stowaway cat? Her bloated body, her flight to an anonymous hotel room? It didn't really matter. She listened to the cat exploring the room and then slept deeply, the events of the birthday party running like an undercurrent beneath her skin.

Something startled Miriam awake. Disoriented, she groped for the light on the bedside table, nearly knocking onto the floor a clock with huge glow-in-the-dark yellow numbers. Remembering where she was, she gave up searching for the light. Persistent knocking. That's what had awakened her.

Struggling to pull herself up onto her elbows, she realized she had been sleeping on her back and felt the fire of heartburn in her chest. On her side she was able to breathe easier, and she concentrated on the whine of the air unit, hoping the person on the other side of the door would simply go away.

Down the middle of the heavy curtains ran a sliver of light that told her it was sunny outside, making the darkness in the room all the more pleasing.

When the door swung open, Miriam leapt out of bed, pulling the bedspread with her as a cover, crying out, "No housekeeping, I don't need anything," all the while scanning the room for Figment.

"You want me to come back later?" Svetlana called from the door.

"Oh! It's you. I didn't know who it was."

"Just me." Svetlana lifted Figment in greeting, holding him expertly by the scruff of the neck. Once she dropped him, he dashed into the bathroom and scrabbled in his litter. "I told the other girls only I take care of this room. You don't worry about anyone coming in."

Miriam sat down on the low dresser that held the television.

"I have fresh towels for you."

"I haven't used any of the others yet."

"No? You sleep this whole time? That's good. Now you should eat."

While Svetlana slipped out of the room to grab something, Miriam hurried into the bathroom. She felt marginally better for having slept so much. On the back of the door hung two white robes of different sizes, and she pulled on the bigger one. Looking in the mirror, she saw deep half moons beneath her eyes.

Svetlana set a plate before her as soon as she sat at the table. *"Pirozhki,"* she explained. "Dumplings. For when you need good food but your stomach must be careful. My daughter loved these when she was pregnant; I made them for her every week."

They were pillows of springy dough baked to a golden brown and stuffed with cabbage, minced vegetables, and meat, tasting of familiar ingredients made foreign. An unlikely breakfast food, yet comforting in their lumpy shape and low spice. Miriam devoured three in quick succession, nervously watching Svetlana make her bed.

"Do you need anything else?" Svetlana asked when she finished.

Miriam shook her head.

"After work, if it's okay with you, I will stop by again."

"If you want to."

"I do. Maybe this morning you can go for a swim. Your body won't ache so much in the water. But not the hot tub. You don't want to boil the baby." The door closed with a quiet scrape against the carpet.

The hotel had two swimming areas: the rectangular pool you'd expect any hotel in America to have, complete with several adults lazily scissor-kicking back and forth; and on the other end of the building, a monumental room with indoor water slides and moats, a bar that served drinks and snacks, and jungle-themed murals painted on every wall.

This pool echoed with the noise of children screaming their way down slides, the splash of fountains, and a soundtrack full of thunder and monkey calls.

At the bar Miriam ordered a large root beer and nachos, feeling sorry for herself when a man next to her ordered a soda and a piece of pizza for his wife.

She settled in a lounge chair where her nachos wouldn't get splashed and opened the notebook she had bought at the gift shop. It was the only one they had, with tan paper and a moose in the upper left-hand corner of every page. When she sketched houses, she usually began inside, with the master bedroom or kitchen determining the layout and general feel of the home. She wondered what would happen if she started outside, with a pool and guesthouse, then worked her way inside the main structure. She set herself the task of creating several designs for a wealthy couple who had money to burn. She tried a kidney-shaped pool, scratched it out, then a rectangle, which she also scratched out. She bent her head to an oddly shaped pool with a fifty-foot long infinity edge that would appear to seamlessly mate water with the sky's horizon. Paul had hated her habit of chewing on pencils when she was thinking, and now, catching herself doing that, she bit down hard, again and again, feeling her sharp eyeteeth sink into the wood.

Just as her ears had grown accustomed to the echoing noise of the pool area, Miriam's eyes had become adept at ignoring the flashes of little bodies running past her chair and the saunter of parents trying to catch up. But when someone walked past on crutches, the slow, awkward movements were different enough that it caught her attention. A mother and daughter. The mother walked slowly, several paces ahead of the daughter, and her face had the pained look of worry etched on it. The daughter leaned heavily on her crutches, and although she didn't have a cast or brace anywhere Miriam could see, she moved her legs as through a mist of pain. She was slender and her jeans and shirt fit with fashionable snugness. Yellowing bruises clustered along one cheek, and as she moved toward the snack bar, placing the tip of each crutch so as to avoid puddles, Miriam saw she was also fighting tears.

"Here," Miriam wanted to say, patting the chair next to her, "sit here. Tell me. Tell me what happened." The desire nearly lifted her out of her chair. But how many people saw her widowed and pregnant state and wanted her to sit and tell them? And how often did it do her, rather than them, any good? They might experience relief that their husbands were still alive and well, or feel pity for her disastrous life, but the weight she carried had so far not been lifted by the process of sharing. Grief was so private that sometimes when she forced herself to respond honestly to "How are you doing?" she felt afterward ashamed, as though she had been foolish to mistake it for a real question.

Yet here she was, wanting desperately to know what had brought this beautiful teenager to a hotel off Highway 90 with bruises that twisted around her neck and disappeared under her collar. Blinking hard, she broke a chip in half and worked the sharp edge through the skin on the cooling nacho cheese, then chewed thirty times, not because her mother had harped at her to do so, but because she seemed to have forgotten how to swallow.

It was early evening when Svetlana stepped into the room again. Miriam was seated at the round table near the glass door, playing solitaire with a new deck of moose-adorned cards. The hotel didn't get the History Channel, so she was watching "NYPD Blue" reruns. The jerky camera movements and pounding music did the job of keeping her from thinking too much. She reached for the remote to turn it off and made room on the table for Svetlana's bags.

"I brought soup."

Miriam watched her ladle servings of the homemade soup—wide noodles, bright vegetables, shredded chicken in a smoky broth. It was steaming. She wondered if Svetlana had gone home after work to make it or if she had warmed it up in a microwave somewhere. A salty, welcoming taste.

Svetlana pulled a chair close, bumping Miriam's knees without self-consciousness, and ripped into a loaf of dark bread with her hands, slathered butter on a chunk, and handed it across the table. That, too, was warm.

"A housekeeper got fired today," Svetlana said easily, as though they ate together all the time and regularly launched directly into conversation. "She was stealing tips. For a week, not a single room I've cleaned had money in it. Today, my manager set trap. Caught her—" she paused, searching for a word. "Red-handed," she finally pronounced, carefully and with some satisfaction. "He gave me sixty dollars bonus. Nice man." She slurped some soup. "You went to the pool today?"

"What was it like, working with Paul?"

Svetlana took the abruptness of this question in stride, but thought a long time before answering. "His eyes were different. I don't mean the blue part. But the way he looked at me, leaning forward, eyes open, seeing. Like I was important. It's a gift, to be a person who truly listens."

"How did he become your lawyer?"

"I was in hospital with broken ribs, and social worker gave me his number. She said I must move into a woman's shelter, but I wasn't sure. Mr. Kovatch convinced me." She dipped her bread in her soup. "And helped me move."

"He did?" Disbelief.

"We had to plan it. The doctor told my husband I would be released from hospital the next day, but really I left sooner. When I knew my husband was at work, Mr. Kovatch and woman from the shelter drove me home to get some things. I had only clothes, but he carried the box for me."

"You didn't take any furniture or anything?"

"No, I didn't want anything. Eh," she shrugged off Miriam's concern. "After my husband sat on couch, it smelled old, like dogs."

Miriam laughed, despite herself. "How did Paul convince you to leave?"

"Do you want short or long answer?"

"Long."

"You eat, I'll talk." Svetlana smiled kindly and pushed her empty bowl away. "It was not always easy for me to say, but I married an abusive man. Most people believe it should be easy for wife to leave abuser. But it's not. I was afraid of him, but I loved him, too. And always I was hoping he would change. I heard a thousand times, 'We can't help you until you help yourself.' Which only made me feel ashamed. Your husband never said anything like that to me, never spoke to me in anger, or telling me what to do as if I'm stupid. Instead, he asked many questions and listened. And he told me what happened to him when he was a little boy."

Miriam spoke through a mouthful of bread. "What do you mean?"

"He told me about the time his mother left his father and went to live with the grandmother." She said this matter-of-factly, obviously expecting this summary to correspond with knowledge Miriam shared.

"This is Paul we're talking about. My husband."

"Yes."

"He told you this?"

"Yes."

"But she didn't leave him. His mom and dad are still together."

"Yes, she went back to him."

"What?" Miriam put down her spoon. Within the space of a few heartbeats she had gone from confusion to disbelief to fear that Svetlana knew something she didn't. "What, exactly, did he tell you?"

"Oh. Let's see. When he was six, his mother left because his father was always saying terrible things to her. Emotional abuse, he called it. They went to live with his grandmother. When his father found out, he kept driving by the house and banging on the door. His grandmother wanted to call police, but his mother didn't because she was too afraid. He promised to change—which my husband always promised, too, after he hurt me—and she went home with him after two days. When they got home, his father said he would kill them both if she ever tried to leave again. He burned Mr. Kovatch's arm to prove he was serious."

"No." Miriam wanted her to stop talking. "It's not true." She knew the scars, had traced the crisscrosses of puckered skin across his right forearm, which he had told her occurred when he accidentally knocked over a pot of boiling water. Her face was betraying her, she knew, revealing that she had not heard this story before. She couldn't bear sitting at the table any longer and got up, but felt trapped, with nowhere to go. Keeping her back to Svetlana, she leaned against the wall just outside the bathroom.

Svetlana had more to say. "Your husband told me that men like this don't deserve families, that they need to be alone with their hatred. But it was his eyes more than his words that gave me the courage to leave. I realized that my husband looked at me with hate. Like I am worm. When Mr. Kovatch looked at me like I am real person, I started to believe that I am deserving more."

Out in the hall, a door slammed and footsteps went pounding by, a child calling to his parents to hurry. From behind her came the sound of Svetlana gathering up the dishes.

"Thank you for dinner, Svetlana," Miriam said, unable to keep her voice steady. She cleared her throat. "I think I'd like to be alone now."

"Your husband was good man."

Miriam nodded and shut herself into the bathroom until Svetlana left.

*r*unning along the outer edge of the enormous water park was a river with a slight current. Lined with fake rocks and murals of climbing ivy and rain forest animals, it moved slowly past the slides and spouting geysers, through a short, dark tunnel, and under a waterfall. A young, embarrassed-looking lifeguard helped Miriam get situated on a large inner tube and gave her a small shove in the right direction. Once the current took her, she was able to move slowly and virtually unnoticed past all the frenetic activity in the echoing space.

On her third revolution around the room, a man's gesture caught her eye, reminding her of Steven. He was standing at the bottom of a slide, apparently waiting for someone to appear there, and as his eyes scanned the water anxiously, his hand alighted on the top of his head, where he smoothed what little hair he had left.

She felt a hitch in her throat, thinking of Steven. Her tube bumped into the wall and she pushed off with her feet. She hated that Joseph knew about his illness before she did. There *had* been signs of it over the years, which she always naively attributed to something else. A lingering cold. Bronchitis he couldn't seem to kick. Even some weight loss . . . how stupid could she be?

"You look like you slimmed down," she had observed the previous summer as he leaned over a small grill on his back porch.

He straightened, turning sideways to show off his profile. "You think?"

"You're not as round as you used to be. Like maybe three months along instead of five," she teased.

"Miriam!" Paul scolded her from his lounge chair.

But rubbing his stomach, Steven had merely laughed. "I prefer to think of it as a Santa Claus look, not a pregnant one."

"Have you been trying to lose weight?"

"Not really." He busied himself with the hamburgers. "A happy accident, I guess."

She didn't think there was anything in this or any other conversation she'd had with him that indicated willful ignorance on her part.

*Maybe I need to start asking everyone if anything bad has happened to them lately,* she thought bitterly. Then at least no one could say she was too self-absorbed to care. Nor would they have an excuse to keep her in the dark.

Back in the hotel room, her toes and fingers pruned, Miriam showered and settled at the table to play solitaire, stopping every so often to interrupt Figment's new game of climbing the curtains. Svetlana had been there; the bed was made, new towels had been laid out, and a large slice of coffee cake was waiting for her. She abandoned the cards and stretched out on the bed. Her fingers were chlorine-scented; when she tucked her hand beneath her damp hair, the smell wafted up.

When she woke, the sun was no longer shining directly into the room, and she had to peel her necklace off her cheek. It had slipped up, imprinting a groove on her skin that she could feel beneath her fingertips. She sat up, mounding the pillows against the headboard in a futile attempt to ward off heartburn.

Unclasping the necklace, she contemplated the engraving of St. Genevieve on the silver medallion. This, her favorite saint, had hung near her heart for years. During elementary school drills, hiding beneath her desk with other Cold War children, Miriam would imagine herself to be Genevieve, the Soviet Union to be Attila the Hun. By her beseeching her fellow classmates to pray, the nuclear missiles would be diverted harmlessly into the already Dead Sea, or when she was feeling particularly heroic, the missiles would arrive but the incinerated would be miraculously restored by her touch.

Miriam couldn't count the number of hours she had spent asking this saint for help. Examining the etched form of the kneeling Genevieve, she tried to quantify the results of her prayers and came up blank. Had she ever received any help—tangible comfort or aid—from this woman who had lived so long ago?

Her mother, who had prayed to countless saints and after whom Miriam had modeled her own spiritual practices, would be horrified by such a question. But what Miriam had always seen as her mother's unwavering faith she now thought could be more accurately defined as fear. Fear, which led her to beg incessantly for mercy.

Miriam set the necklace on the bedside table, where it sat in a disorderly pile of chain links.

When Svetlana let herself into the room later that evening, Miriam pretended to be asleep, and the woman slipped out quietly, leaving food behind.

The next day was a restless one, spent wandering the halls and various play areas, until, back in the room, Miriam stared alternately at the television and out the window at the acres of parking lots and buildings surrounding the hotel. The shadows lengthened with excruciating slowness, and when at last she heard the door open, she greeted Svetlana's voice with eagerness and not a little embarrassment for her behavior of the past few days.

Before she could think of a way to apologize, Svetlana announced, *"Kotlety Pozharskie,"* unpacking a bag, her tongue flowing smoothly over the sounds Miriam couldn't begin to identify.

"What did you say?" she asked as Mei might have.

"Chicken," was the explanation. Svetlana scooped a patty onto Miriam's plate. "My mother's recipe." She opened another bowl, revealing a mound of glistening spinach.

"In Russian. How do you say it again?"

Her inquiry seemed to please Svetlana. *"Kot-let-y Po-zhar-skie,"* she pronounced clearly, laughing when Miriam was unable to repeat it after numerous tries.

"I think Russian is too hard for Americans. Much harder than English. We learn your language in our schools, when we're young, but Russian is so hard your children don't even try it."

"You're probably right," Miriam agreed, though she guessed there were other reasons Americans had for not learning Russian.

The chicken had apparently been ground, mixed with bread crumbs, and then fried. She took small bites, unsure how the grease would affect her.

"You know, you don't have to bring dinner every night," Miriam said. "I'm sure you're tired after working all day and I could order room service."

Svetlana shrugged. "Is no trouble. You're better company than a living room with no couch."

The spinach was unusually tart, as though it had been drizzled with vinegar. It tasted only slightly better than it looked, slopped on the plate. She choked it down, thinking, *these nutrients are for you, babe.*

Svetlana served herself seconds and pushed another chicken patty onto Miriam's plate although she hadn't finished the first. "So." Svetlana cleared her throat. "You have been thinking, yes? Why your husband didn't tell you the same things he told me about his family?"

Miriam nodded, enormously relieved that Svetlana had brought it up. "I've been trying to figure out why, but I just can't understand it. That burn on his arm? He told me it was an accident. He never hinted that his dad did it deliberately."

Svetlana looked thoughtful but didn't offer any explanations.

"I didn't even know that he worked with women's shelters until I met you. Why would he keep that a secret from me?"

Svetlana took a sip of water. "One time Vasili, my husband, beat me with hammer. The back part of it." She held two fingers up, slightly curled, like claws. "I was already living at shelter, which he didn't know the location of, but somehow he found out where I was working at a restaurant, washing dishes. He waited for me one night after I finish work and since I wouldn't get in his car, I went to hospital instead."

Miriam tried not to look shocked by the story or by the matter-of-fact tone in which it was being conveyed. No discernable anger or bitterness.

"I was in hospital when Mr. Kovatch came to get pictures of my injuries in case we needed to go to trial. The police couldn't find Vasili to arrest him, but he showed up in my room, crying, saying he loved me and was so sorry. Your husband calmed him down and waited with me until the police arrived. I knew it was right thing to do, but afterwards I cried, too. Because I know Vasili loves me, even now. And I love him. But to be with him is impossible, so my heart breaks. Some people say, 'Your husband hit you so you're stupid to keep loving him.' But not *your* husband. He never said anything like that."

Although Miriam could picture Paul's compassion in this situation, it killed her that she had, while he was still alive, acted as if he were not capable of such things unless she were a witness to it. She put her fork down and clasped her hands tightly around her belly.

"If he told you about this when it happened," Svetlana asked, "what would you have done?"

Miriam shook her head, watching Figment crawl onto the woman's lap.

"You would have worried about him, yes?"

"Of course," she admitted. It stood to reason he encountered other violent men like Vasili, acting as a buffer between them and the women they were abusing.

"You would have wanted him to stop?"

"No." She knew this absolutely.

"Would you have worried about me? Or the other women at the shelter?"

Miriam's gaze moved from Svetlana's hand caressing Figment to her eyes. "Yes."

The Russian nodded.

"I would've wanted to get involved."

"Perhaps your husband thought it was not possible."

She pushed Figment off her lap gently and excused herself to go to the bathroom.

Miriam packed away the dishes. A high number of abused children grow up to be abusers themselves, she knew. Paul had managed, somehow, to break this pattern. Perhaps part of his strategy involved keeping her out of it, as if the very mention would make abuse a factor in their relationship.

But, no. The truth came like a landslide. She would have viewed the women and children in the shelter as mere projects that could endear her to God by giving her the opportunity to do good. She had always believed that others perceived her as she wanted to see herself: as a self-sacrificing and giving person, always on hand to relieve the burdens of others. The self-delusion now popped like a balloon in her chest, radiating real pain.

She remembered something infuriating Paul had said to her years before. She had complained that she had missed out on the opportunity to go to college because she had to take care of her mother for so many years. "At least now you get to play the martyr," he had said. "College couldn't have given you that."

She wanted to cry, thinking now that he had seen her with such clarity and loved her still.

That night, she dreamed of the o'o', an extinct bird Esther had once described to her in graphic detail. Miriam was kneeling in a field of tall, yellowing grass, raising binoculars to her eyes carefully so as to not make a rustling sound. Her breath was audible as she searched for movement in a distant tree whose shape and contours she knew like the face of a best friend. Adjusting the focus, she had a sinking premonition that the last o'o', who had been calling desperately for the past four years to a mate that did not exist, had not survived the storm.

The island foliage looked like it had been whipped hard. Leaves that hadn't been stripped from the tree looked tattered; branches were flung about. She gave up her silent vigil and began walking, her pant legs growing heavy with moisture.

There, under the tree that had once held the empty nest, was a body. Brown feathers, yellow thighs. Sleek and dead, its beak open. She used a trowel to dig a grave, listening to the metal slice into the earth. When she was finally able to lay the slack but curiously heavy body into the hole and pack the dirt firm on top of it, she sat back on her heels in relief. No more hoarse nights, wondering why a mate didn't respond to his cries.

"It's better this way," she whispered and then woke, trying to wipe mud from her fingers onto the starchy hotel sheets.

The baby thrummed softly with hiccoughs inside her.

Svetlana burst into her room the following day in high spirits. "Today we celebrate," she announced, hefting a bottle of champagne with flourish, nearly dropping one of her bags of groceries and having to shuffle awkwardly the rest of the way to the table. "My special breakfast: *blini* with sour cream. For you, also I put on strawberries. When you try these, your mouth will never be so happy in its life." She plugged in a portable burner and wiped a small frying pan with oil.

"What's the occasion?"

"Many reasons. My husband is no longer my husband. He's in Russia and has no permission to return. But mostly, I paid my own rent today with no help from the shelter or anyone else. Soon I will save enough to buy furniture that does not smell like dog-man." Svetlana's eyes gleamed as she twisted the gold band off her finger. "Watch," she ordered, digging in one of the bags before stepping outside the sliding glass door with a hammer in hand. She hunched down on the sidewalk, and after grinning at Miriam, swung her arm wide to take a great whack at the ring lying in front of her. It shot out from under the hammer and bounced off the hood of a car, and Svetlana went scrambling after it, pounding away as soon as she laid hands on it again.

At first taken aback, Miriam was helpless with laughter. Listening to Svetlana's exclamations, she was struck by how unforced her cheer was. There was no edge to her joy, like the sharp undercurrents that emanated from Esther when she drank because she could, because she had once again gotten her period, her laughter merely covering the pain of a body unable to stay pregnant. Esther was on her way to becoming a bitter woman, Miriam thought with surprise, wiping her eyes as Svetlana stepped back into the room, sweating from her effort but smiling broadly.

Svetlana popped the cork on the champagne and pressed a glass into Miriam's hand. Her warnings about what was bad for the baby were apparently limited to hot tubs and cleaning fumes.

Svetlana raised her glass in a toast. "To the INS, for deporting poor bastard."

It seemed a toast worth joining in, pregnancy or no. Miriam allowed the bubbles to touch her tongue.

"It is the right word: bastard?"

"I'm certain of it."

Svetlana nodded in satisfaction. "Yes, it feels on my tongue like the right word. He was bastard. I learned it at the shelter, and many other words, too, but this one is my favorite."

Miriam wondered about the family that Svetlana had left behind. "You said you have a daughter?"

"Two. And one granddaughter."

"You must miss them very much."

"I do. Someday." She busied herself over the hot pan, spreading in it a thin layer of batter and swirling it around, flipping the pancake the minute the edges began to brown and curl. "Someday they will visit me. But it's an adventure to be in United States. Did you know, you can go to the library and use the computers? I have e-mail, so we talk all the time, which makes it easier to be so far away." She slid the pancake onto a plate and filled it with strawberry preserves and dollops of sour cream before rolling it with a flash of her spatula.

Under her expectant gaze, Miriam tried the pancake, surprised by the tangy perfection of fruit and sour cream, a combination she would never have dared on her own.

Her face must have registered pleasure, because Svetlana grinned.

Through a full mouth, Miriam said, "I have furniture you could have."

"Oh, no. Thank you. I will buy."

"No, really. I'm selling the house that Paul and I lived in and am planning to move into a much smaller one. I've kept the furniture so the rooms won't look too empty when the Realtor shows the house, but once it sells, there's a lot of stuff I want to get rid of. There's a double bed in the guest room and a dresser. A couch and entertainment center. A television, too. Do you have a television?"

"No, no, is too much."

"I've got three televisions. One in the den, one in the living room, and a small one in the basement where Paul used to work out. What do I need three televisions for?"

Svetlana said uncertainly, "I don't know about that." She draped another *blini* on Miriam's plate. "I don't want you feeling sorry for me."

"I don't." Miriam realized it was true. "Oh, these are so good, I want to lick the plate."

"Go ahead, I won't look."

"So, *do* you?"

"Do I what?"

"Have a television?"

"No."

"Once I sell the house, I'll call you. I'd really love for you to have the furniture. That's so much better than giving it to Goodwill. You should come over and look it over first. If you think the couch is hideous and don't want it, I won't be offended, I promise."

"You mentioned a bed?"

"Yup," Miriam's head snapped up. "You don't have a bed?"

Svetlana shook her head.

"Oh, Svetlana. You might have a strong back, but sleeping on the floor can't be good for your body after a day of cleaning. I'll call you right away, as soon as I get home. I don't need to keep it until the house sells; who knows how long that's going to take. My brother has a truck, so we'll bring it over to you."

Svetlana turned away, but not before Miriam saw that her eyes had brimmed. "I would like to clean your house for you once a week." Miriam started to object, but Svetlana cut her off with a wave of her spatula. "I told you. Bending over tub, breathing fumes. Is not good for the baby."

"Okay," she agreed, quietly. "I could use the help."

As Svetlana gathered her things to go, she paused and said simply, "You will not be here tomorrow, will you?"

Miriam was startled. She looked through the window, where the sun glinted off the windshield of a car. "You're right," she said. "I need to go home."

Svetlana took a seat next to her on the bed. "I want to give you this," she said, pulling something out of her pocket. "There is a beach at home that I go to with my family on vacation. White, white sand, bright in your eyes, and blue water." Her hands fluttered as though tracing the movement of rolling waves. "That sound, of water going back and forth, it is like being rocked by the hand of God." She opened her fingers and revealed a small stone.

"Years ago, I went to this beach alone, when I was going through dark time. Much like you, I needed to get away, to be quiet. Two things I needed to know." She ticked them off her fingers. "One, is life worth living." She paused and Miriam's heart leapt, like a small thrill, to hear it put so plainly. "And two, is God good."

Miriam looked down at her hands, steadied her breath.

"Every night, before bed, I sweep porch and front steps of cabin to get off all the sand, so it's clean in morning when I go out there to eat breakfast. But one time, I open the door and this rock is on top step, sitting there, waiting to tell me something."

Miriam accepted the rock, which fit perfectly against her palm. It was a dark, oval stone, almost black, with splotches of green that cupped the light when she tilted it toward the window.

"The rocks on shore are white or brown, nothing special. Nothing like this."

The surface of the rock was absolutely smooth, as though someone had worried away all its rough edges.

"I don't know why, but it made me think of English poem I learn by heart." She paused and closed her eyes to recite. "'But still I felt like a long shore on which all the waves of pain of all the world were beating. My Father drew near and said, There is only one shore long enough for that. Upon My Love, that long, long shore, those waves are beating now; but you can have fellowship with Me.'"

Svetlana pushed off the bed wearily and turned toward Miriam. "Sometimes you can only lift your arms to God, helpless. You hold onto this"— she closed Miriam's fingers around the stone. "Until you are strong again, I have faith for both of us."

After Svetlana left, moving quickly through the door to keep Figment from escaping into the hallway, Miriam curled up on the bed, not moving to turn on a light until long after the sun had gone down.

# eighteen

*W*hen Miriam arrived at home, she listened to her messages while letting Figment out of his cage. The sound of the first voice made her cringe: Frank, from the grief support group, inviting her to have dinner and watch a movie with his girls.

"Come hungry," he said, eagerly, and whereas once she might have been repulsed by his naïve belief that watching her eat would somehow cure his daughters, now she felt sorrow over the depth of his helplessness. She wished there was something real she could offer him, but despite his reassurances that it wouldn't be a date, she didn't think his daughters would view it as anything but. She knew she had no interest in a relationship with Frank, but perhaps they could get together for coffee periodically. Be a mini support group of two. She would call and offer, anyway.

Figment tore out of the kitchen with his tail puffed, claws scrabbling on the tile.

The Realtor was next, to say a couple had seen the house several times and made an OFFER. "I left it on the kitchen counter in a purple folder. I think you'll like what you see!"

Steven's first message was concerned but light in tone, wanting to know if she "was okay after that debacle of a birthday party."

His next messages were increasingly sober and succinct, ending with a teeth-gritted "I can't believe you've done this."

The phone rang and Miriam leapt to pick it up.

"Hey! You're there!" exclaimed Suzi. "You won't believe it, but not only do we have a motivated buyer for YOUR house, but, hear the drum roll, I know of a house that's going on the market this VERY morning that I know you'll just LOVE. It's on the EXACT same block as your brother's house, but we've GOT to get over there right away before someone else snatches it up."

"I just got home from a trip—"

"Listen. It's a Cape Cod with REAL brick and a REAL fireplace and it's in GREAT condition. Did I mention it's in the EXACT neighborhood you wanted? I expect them to get two or three offers before the day's up. Can you meet me there in half an hour?"

Figment was still running from room to room, skidding on the rug in the bathroom, pausing momentarily and then launching himself once again.

She picked up her car keys, jangled them a few times, and headed out.

Suzi was right. The house was perfect. If Miriam couldn't design and build her own home, this was the next best thing. A sense of familiarity followed her through the rooms, and she ignored each item of the current owners' furniture as if they were mere imposters. Wood floors throughout, an open kitchen with glassed-in breakfast nook, beautifully sloped ceilings on the second floor. The smaller of the two bedrooms had shelves built into the eaves that Miriam could imagine filled with a small lamp, books, and stuffed animals.

She agreed to offer the owners what they were asking since Suzi was positive they'd have other offers soon. It was probably a foolish decision that Paul would not have made, but he was noticeably absent. The Realtor was ecstatic. "You are going to be SO happy here," she predicted through her rolled-down window as she sped off to finish the paperwork.

Leaving her car in the driveway, Miriam walked the half block to her brother's house, appreciating the trees shading the street and the sidewalk that periodically buckled over their roots. Difficult to navigate on a bike, but she liked the evidence of nature fighting back, of ruining the pretense of a smooth surface.

Turning to look back at the house, she felt as though she had just witnessed a small miracle. The eternally optimistic Suzi had nevertheless not been optimistic about finding a house here and had urged her repeatedly to expand the search geographically. When Miriam first set her sights on this neighborhood, it had been a gut feeling, but her decision now seemed nearly prophetic. Someday Steven would need her to be this close. *That is, if he needs anyone other than Joseph,* she caught herself thinking resentfully, and felt chagrined. If Joseph stood by Steven even through illness, she had no right to be anything other than glad for them both.

Although she hadn't expected an answer when she knocked on Steven's front door, Joseph appeared almost immediately, clutching a sheaf of paper and a red pen. It was apparent that he had been working.

"Miriam," he said with some shock, taking off his reading glasses. "Come in, come in," and as he opened the screen door and stepped aside for her, she knew his relationship with Steven had crossed into new territory.

"Steven's in his studio, working," he said.

Miriam caught his sleeve as he turned toward the living room where she saw more paper strewn on the couch and coffee table. "How is he?"

He searched her face, and she wasn't able to tell if the intensity in his eyes, the furrow of his brows, was anger, concern, or simply a struggle to find the right words.

"It's okay," she said, letting him off the hook.

When Miriam walked into Steven's studio, he was ripping orange and brown checked material off a sofa, using a screwdriver to pry up old staples. He stopped abruptly when he saw her.

She smiled uncertainly, started to say something, but lost her nerve.

"You won't believe the hell I've been through," he said in a terrible voice. He swiped at his upper lip with the side of his wrist. "I've called hospitals. I've searched the papers every day for accidents. I've been to your house at least twice a day. I had no idea where you were."

"I went on a trip," she said, her voice feeble. "To a hotel."

When he didn't respond, she added ridiculously, "It had a big moose."

"Six days. You were gone for six days. I'm on a first-name basis with the police in your suburb."

She felt the weight of his anger as he spread his palms flat on the workbench and leaned against them. Despite herself, her defenses rose. "That's a bit of an overreaction, isn't it, Steven? Calling the police? And hospitals? In case you haven't noticed, I'm not a child anymore and you're not my babysitter. Are you saying I need to check in with you every time I leave town?"

"How was I to know you didn't drive off the road somewhere or go to some hotel to end it all?"

She was scornful. "You can't really believe I would do that."

"Really." He waited for her to meet his gaze. "The night you left, you had been given a present from your dead husband, you and your best friend had a terrible fight, and you found out that I'm HIV positive. Before that, you were barely hanging on as it was."

The hardness collapsed inside her, a sensation not unlike falling. She looked away. "Well, when you put it like that."

He picked up the screwdriver and wrenched another staple from the sofa. Dust and bits of cotton fibers danced in the air as he ripped the fabric away from the wooden frame. A cough caught him off-guard, and he buried his face in the crook of his arm. She took a few steps toward him but he stopped her with an upheld hand.

When he regained his breath, he said, "Your in-laws were here."

"Their visit. I—oh, God." She steadied herself against the workbench. "I forgot."

"You forgot."

"They called about a month ago to tell me their travel plans, but I hadn't talked to them since. I can't believe I completely spaced it. I'm sorry Steven, I—"

"They didn't feel comfortable staying at your house without you there, so they stayed here. I wouldn't want to be you, when you have to explain to Henry what happened."

"How long were they here?"

"One night. They got up the next morning, refused Joseph's omelets, I guess because they put two and two together, and took a cab to the airport."

*I'm sorry* was so inadequate she didn't bother saying it. She had always worked so hard to not offend or anger anyone, and since Paul's death, she had succeeded in not much else. An elbow jabbed at her from within, and she felt a blaze of fear, that she had made the wrong decision, even with this. *What sort of damage will I do to you?* She slipped her hand beneath her shirt, pressing against the tightness of her belly.

Steven attacked another staple.

After watching him work for what felt like forever and at a complete loss for words, she left the studio and skirted the main house so she wouldn't run into Joseph.

Back at the house she had just bought, she peered into the small entryway, where a coat rack fit snugly into the corner. There was room for a chest, too, for boots and mittens, she thought.

In back, she noted again the glassed-in breakfast nook, this time without pleasure. As she tiptoed to look through her reflection into the kitchen, the baby suddenly jolted, placing what felt like twenty pounds of pressure directly on her bladder.

"Stop it," she cried, trying to shift the baby into a better position and hurriedly checking the back door in the off chance Suzi had left it unlocked. With rising panic, she realized that even if she were to jump into the car, she wouldn't be able to hold it long enough to get anywhere. Her options were ridiculously limited. She couldn't go back to Steven's, not yet. She could knock on a neighbor's door and explain that she was buying this house and, oh, by the way, can I use your bathroom NOW?

The backyard had thick hedges on all sides that were filling out with spring foliage, but she could still see through them into adjoining yards. It looked as though the neighbors on either side were gone; she hadn't seen any vehicles or movement in all the time she'd been there.

Her stomach severely limited her ability to crouch, but she had a skirt on, so out of desperation, she shimmied out of her underpants, hiked up the skirt, and peed in the flowerbed, using the house as support against her back.

*So this is what my life has come to.*

Unable to face returning to an empty house, Miriam decided to take a chance and visit Father Jake. His face registered surprise when she peeked around his door, and as he pulled off his reading glasses, transitioned to shock when she stepped into his office and he took in her pregnant state.

"You've had your hands full, haven't you?" he observed, and before the sentence was out, Miriam was crying.

His office was in its usual state of disarray, with books and paper piled on every surface. He started to clear a chair for her, but in his haste, papers and magazines cascaded onto the floor. Throwing his hands in the air, he led her to an adjoining room, to a broken-down, lumpy couch where he sat next to her, his nearness as much as his words further undoing her.

He didn't try to hurry or shush her, but simply let her cry.

She worked hard to compose herself. "I don't know what to say," she finally managed to get out.

"Anything," he said, his voice low.

Still, she struggled to know how to begin. With making an appointment for an abortion? With wanting to rail at God for taking Paul? For having all her good intentions exposed as something worse than flawed?

"I'm sorry I haven't called or come to see you before this," she said. "I didn't have the energy to do much of anything. Plus, there were so many things going through my head that I couldn't have put into words even if I'd wanted to, and—" She stopped, became absorbed in folding her tissue into a tight square.

"And?" he prompted.

She flicked her eyes toward him, then back at the tissue. "I'm so ashamed about the funeral," she whispered.

He leaned toward her, making no movement to speak, and she slowly regained control.

"When you left that message on my answering machine," she continued, "you said Henry put me in an impossible situation. But that's not really true, is it?"

"I think it is true."

"No," she shook her head. "He asked me to choose between him and my faith. And I chose him because I was afraid. As if what he thinks is more important than what you or God think. Even Steven was disappointed in me."

He started to respond, but she interrupted him. "Nothing you say will convince me that what I did was okay."

He closed his mouth and nodded thoughtfully. "Okay," he said. "It may not have been the right choice, but it was understandable, given the circumstances."

She shrugged dismissively.

"Don't underestimate the difficulty of the situation you were in. Paul's death was a shocking blow. You were off-kilter to begin with, and when you add the unreasonable and angry demands of a parent who should be your advocate, not your enemy, I think it's safe to say your response was understandable. And very human."

"St. Genevieve would have done the right thing, no matter what."

"Yeah, well," he said wryly, "we're not all called to be martyrs. Besides. Even more to the point, you haven't done anything unforgivable."

Her hand sought out the necklace of St. Genevieve she no longer wore. Might as well get it all out. "I should probably tell you that I can't remember the last time I prayed."

"Okay," he nodded, completely unruffled.

"I always tried so hard to be like my mother, you know? But now, when I think about it, what did all her prayers really accomplish? Every day she pleaded with God, but that never stopped anything bad from happening. And even though I *knew* that, I still followed her example, somehow expecting that God would spare me even though he never spared her." She blew her nose.

"Perhaps you're right to question your mother's piety."

This was unexpected. "You think my mother was pious?" She understood he did not use the term positively.

"I think your mother tried to use her faith as a bargaining chip. She wasn't alone in that, of course. At some point, most of us are probably guilty of the same thing. We want health or wealth or success, or like your mother, safety from pain, and we try to figure out a way to finagle it from God."

"So we shouldn't pray for any of those things?"

"No, I don't mean that. I'm confident it pleases God when we pour out our hearts to Him about anything and everything. But . . ." He squinched his lips to the side and chewed the inside of his cheek as he always did when he was thinking hard. "But prayer also involves listening. Maybe your inability to pray right now means that you're learning this."

"Maybe," Miriam allowed, unconvinced. Then: "I don't really understand any of it."

"Sometimes, to be honest, I don't either."

"Take that back," she said. "You're supposed to understand everything."

He laughed.

She took a deep breath. "Will you hear my confession?"

"Absolutely."

*a*fter peeking into Steven's studio window to make sure

he was there, Miriam rang the doorbell and fled, cutting

through his neighbor's backyard so he wouldn't see her
If she were not pregnant and if they were not fighting, she
would have paused to laugh at herself and spy on his
reaction to the dozen yellow roses she had left for him.

She was glad to be rid of the flowers. Their cloying
scent, which she had never really cared for, had saturated
her skin and lungs, nearly choking her on the drive from
the florists.

*All for love,* she thought, hurrying across the street to
where her car was parked and trying not to lumber from
side to side. Walking, especially walking fast, seemed less

and less dignified the longer the pregnancy wore on. She hated to think what the next few months would be like.

The interior of the car was still rose-drenched, so she sank into the front seat but left the door open to air it out.

She needed time to catch her breath before mustering the strength for errands. There was so much to do. Doctor visits, meetings with the Realtor and mortgage lender, home inspections, and packing. Thanks to Svetlana, some cleaning was already done. Embarrassing what a person discovered under beds and bureaus that had been stationary for years. Cat fur and dust bunnies the size of her fist. Buttons, a broken comb, pennies, a crusty, balled-up sock, and a chipped guitar pick, though to the best of her knowledge, the house had never had a guitar in it.

She had discovered her mother's rosary, too, buried under computer manuals in the office closet, and was surprised when she didn't feel relief or comfort upon caressing the familiar wooden beads. In fact, she had felt entirely neutral.

She turned the car on and cranked the air-conditioner, still leaving the door ajar. Exhaustion was creeping up as steadily as the summer heat. Each morning, after a restless and uncomfortable night, she woke to the long day thinking there would surely be enough time to get everything done. Time, yes. Energy, no.

A cardinal made its upward sweeping call from a bush near the front door of the house. Miriam closed her eyes, listening.

The unmistakable noise of someone opening the passenger door startled Miriam so much she hollered. Steven plopped down in the seat, looking pleased with himself. Adrenaline sizzled along her limbs.

"Where on earth," she gasped, "did you come from?"

"Well, you see, there's this thing called a sperm. And when the sperm finds an egg—"

"Oh, shut up," she groaned.

"Speaking of where we came from, how old were you when you found the book?"

Her mind scrambled to follow. "What are you talking about?"

"The book. About the birds and the bees that Mom conveniently hid in strategic places so she wouldn't have to say the word *sex* out loud."

Miriam giggled.

"I was seven," he said. "It was in the end table by the television, buried under a mountain of newspapers, which Mom had told me to throw away. It had eye-popping illustrations, if I remember correctly."

"I found it in second grade on the shelf with Mom's cookbooks. I waited until the middle of the night to go get it so I could read it under my covers with a flashlight. I was terrified Mom was going to catch me."

"An interesting read, though it didn't make much sense to me at the time. Still doesn't, now that I think about it."

"I haven't thought of that book in years."

"Is that how you're going to break the news about procreation to your progeny? Leave a book out for him or her to read guiltily and under cover of darkness?"

"The kid's not even born yet and you're talking about sex education? That's just what I need. One more thing to worry about."

Steven idly drummed the dashboard.

The cardinal streaked past the windshield, a flurry of red.

"You know," Steven said. "It's the strangest thing. I just received a dozen roses from someone. 'With love from your rotten sister,' I believe the note read. You know anything about that?"

"I'm amazed," Miriam exclaimed, widening her eyes. "I didn't realize Theresa knew she was rotten."

He gave a bark of laughter. "So you just happen to be hiding in some stranger's driveway near my house at the exact moment they're delivered."

"Actually, it's not a stranger's house."

"You getting cozy with my neighbors?"

"No, I'm *becoming* your neighbor."

"That's a frightening thought. An old man with halitosis and liver spots lives here."

She lifted her chin toward the house. "It's mine."

He searched her face. "What?"

"Mmm-hmm. I move in a couple weeks."

He made an astonished sound. "But it's not for sale."

"Not anymore, it's not. I bought it the day it went on the market. They never bothered with a sign."

"When'd this happen?"

"The day I got back from the hotel."

This silenced him, and they both sat looking at the house.

She touched his wrist. "I never asked if you wanted a sister living so close to you."

His lips moved slowly into a smirk. "I don't mind so long as she's rotten."

"That could probably be arranged."

"Well." He looked at his watch. "You want to grab some lunch? I have a hankering for a Potbelly sandwich and barbecue potato chips."

"Does that mean I'm forgiven?"

He smiled sadly at her. "Only if I am."


Although it seemed stupid to purchase anything before the move, Miriam decided it would be better to have a few more boxes to haul than to trust she'd have the energy to go shopping later.

To her relief, everyone, including Theresa and Jenny, had honored her request to not have a baby shower; perhaps she had the disastrous birthday party to thank for that.

She pushed her cart resolutely toward the back of the store, expecting to feel as overwhelmed by diapers, burp rags, and pacifiers as she had been by maternity clothes. But once she touched a blanket with smooth, brushed cotton and traced the delicate stitching on a Winnie the Pooh quilt, she felt a sort of giddiness come over her.

The ultrasound tech had told her it was a boy, but she stayed away from primary blue colors, choosing instead bright yellow or white blankets, neutral sleepers, white undershirts. Colors that could go either way.

Here was a packet of little finger puppets. A duck, turtle, kitten, and puppy, all fuzzy and pastel with happy grins on their faces that made her want to talk in a high-pitched voice to her belly.

Theresa had told her that she couldn't have too many socks. No wonder, she thought, reaching for a pack of six. They were impossibly small. She would probably lose several between here and the checkout, let alone in the washer and dryer at home.

She was standing beside her full cart, trying to understand the difference between the various breast pumps, when a man's voice said, "Hey, I think I know you."

She looked over her shoulder, embarrassed.

"Frank, from the grief support group," he reminded her unnecessarily, making a gesture like a limp salute. "I almost didn't recognize you at first with your hair pulled back."

Miriam's hand fluttered up to her hair, which she had pulled into a jumbled bun to keep her neck cool. *He couldn't have approached me when I was looking at baby name books.*

"It looks good that way," he said.

"Oh, thanks," she said. "I'm sorry I never got back to you about a Friday night movie."

"When you didn't even come back to the group, I thought I must've scared you off."

"No," she said, only half-lying. "I was out of town when you left a message for me and I've been busy getting ready to move, but—" before she could offer to meet him for coffee sometime, he interrupted.

"No biggie. I'm here to pick up some stuff for my girl-friend," he said, leaning on "girlfriend" as if he were still practicing the word.

"Yeah?"

"She's from Idaho. I met her in a chat room three weeks ago and we've been instant messaging and talking on the phone every day since then. I'm going to the airport right after this. She's visiting for three days, and I wanted to buy some scented candles and nice-smelling shampoo. You have any suggestions?"

Miriam shook her head. "Don't you think she'll bring her own shampoo?"

He blinked a few times.

"Wow, three weeks," she said in a tone she hoped he would mistake for admiration. "That's pretty quick."

"When you know what you're looking for, why wait?"

"How do you know it's really a woman?"

He laughed. "We've sent each other pictures. Plus we've talked on the phone for hours. It'd be pretty hard to fake her voice. Between you and me, I was relieved when I saw her picture because I was afraid she'd be too skinny. I mean, she's not obese or anything, but I needed to make sure she wasn't a skeleton. I told her right off the bat that my only absolute requirement is that she not have an eating disorder, but you never can tell until you actually see a person."

"Right," Miriam smiled weakly. "How are your girls doing?"

"Oh, I don't know. I think it's impossible for parents to tell. It's not like they really talk to me about anything, and whenever I bring up the idea of getting into counseling, they scream and cry so much that I drop it." He shrugged, a helpless gesture. "What can you do?"

She hoped that if she were in his position, she'd be able to think of a few things. And if one approach didn't work, that she'd have the insight to try something different. "Are they still counting calories?"

"Probably. But they're not talking about it in front of me, which I guess is a good sign. What about you?" he asked, clearly ready for a different topic. "Did you get remarried?"

"No," she said, mystified by the question.

He gestured at her stomach.

"Oh, that. No, I had just gotten pregnant when my husband died."

He plucked a red-striped rattle shaped like a donut from her cart, turned it over in his hands a few times. "I see you're out getting supplies. Don't forget nail clippers. The ones for adults are too big. And you can never have enough pacifiers. You're always losing one, and you don't want to be hunting around in the middle of the night when the little monster is screaming."

Miriam stared at him in amazement. "Thanks for the advice."

Frank put the rattle back in her cart. "Well," he said, checking his watch. "I think I'll get some Pantene. That smells good, doesn't it? It was nice seeing you again, Miriam."

She watched him disappear into the housewares department, nearly laughing aloud with relief, feeling as though she had narrowly missed a train wreck.

His poor girls. He wasn't just baffled by them, he appeared to not want to go the extra mile in order to connect with them. Not that she imagined they made it easy for him. She shuddered to think what challenges lay before her, and sometimes, especially in the middle of the night, she felt nearly paralyzed with fear that even if Paul were alive, she still wouldn't be up to the task.

"God help me," she sighed, placing her palms flat on her stomach and waiting patiently until she felt movement before turning back to the breast pumps.

She had left a message of apology for disappearing for several days on Henry and Martha's answering machine without receiving any response. To apologize again struck her as groveling, and she didn't yet know exactly how to incorporate her new knowledge of Paul's childhood into their current relationship. She decided to send a letter, giving them her new address, telling them she felt the baby moving every day now, and reminding them that they were going to be the only grandparents her child had. What they did with that would be entirely up to them. After the baby was born, they were welcome to visit, she wrote. "Just call me a few weeks in advance and I'll make reservations for you at a hotel near my house."

Marveling at her nerve, she slipped the murky picture from her ultrasound into the card and sealed the envelope.

Of course, there was still the very real possibility that even if they got past this conflict, Henry would become more controlling and abusive without Paul there to keep him in line. With a child to protect, she'd have to trust that she'd find the strength to make sure he was not a toxic presence in their lives.

"God help me," she said a second time that week, and realized it was the most authentic prayer she had uttered in a long time.

## twenty

$S$he got up early the day of the move, her mind already racing with details of what needed to happen when. Steven was picking up the rental truck, Carl and Theresa were bringing coffee, and the fridge held cans of soda since it was supposed to be a blistering hot day: upper eighties and humid.

Mrs. Harmel had eagerly offered to bring over a pan of her famous cinnamon rolls in the morning. Miriam was surprised at how disappointed her neighbor was about her moving away.

Ever since the funeral, Miriam had been taking baths, but today she leaned into the Love Cave and turned the water on, full blast, stepping in when the temperature was as cool as she could stand it.

The stone tiles were rough beneath her fingers, sending memories pulsing along her nerves. She turned slowly, feeling the water stream down her skin, then stood facing Paul's side of the dual shower. She reached over and turned on his faucet, doing a little dance when the water splashed too cold on her feet.

As it warmed, she wished he was standing there, shampooing his hair at the same time as her, grinning at how long it took her to rinse the suds from her heavy curls.

"Come on, slowpoke, what's the holdup?" He'd reach for the soap, rubbing it over his body frantically, as if they were in a dead heat for home, then linger, watching her.

As much as she tried not to, she was forgetting him. Whether he gestured large or kept his elbows near his body, the exact way his lips and eyes animated his face, the cadence of his voice. All these details were losing their definition, as if he were a pencil sketch smudging under her thumb.

How much more would she lose him in a new home he had never seen? When he had never left this cupboard door open every time he went for a glass or left that toilet seat up? A terrible form of buyer's remorse set in, and after her shower, she dabbed shadow on her eyelids in an attempt to disguise their puffiness.

As she took a last look around the bedroom, her eyes lighted on the rock Svetlana had given her. She reached for it on the bedside table, feeling again how perfectly it fit her palm. She slipped it into her pocket for safekeeping.

Mrs. Harmel arrived before anyone else and didn't require much persuading to stay for a while. She perched on a stool at the kitchen island, and Miriam stood across from her, pulling apart a cinnamon roll and eating it with her fingers. She felt in a hurry to get to work, but could tell Mrs. Harmel wanted to talk.

"Do you know anything about the people who bought your house?"

"It's a family. The parents are in their forties and they have three kids, all under the age of ten. Two boys and a girl. It'll be a lot more interesting than having me around."

Mrs. Harmel chattered about all the different people who had moved in and out of the neighborhood, gossiping about her favorite topic: the bohemian couple who had a teenager on drugs. Miriam waved to the parents periodically on her way to get the mail, but had never spoken directly to them. All her information came from Mrs. Harmel's regular updates, which she realized with a pang she would miss.

From the front of the house came the beeping of a truck backing up. Steven, Ben, Theresa, and Carl all arrived at the same time. Crowding into the kitchen, they greeted Mrs. Harmel, and Carl pressed a cup of coffee into her hands. She sat, bright-eyed and perfectly happy to be in the middle of all the activity, probably gathering tales to tell other neighbors.

Theresa quickly whipped them into orderly robots of efficiency, sending the men to load the biggest pieces of furniture onto the truck while she finished packing the dishes. Miriam put Figment into his carrier so he wouldn't get stepped on and then worked on emptying the refrigerator, filling several coolers with perishables and ice.

A cell phone on the counter chimed loudly, and Theresa said, "Is that Ben's? Ben," she hollered. "Your phone!"

"No, it's mine," Miriam corrected, wiping her hands.

"How about that. Welcome to the twenty-first century," Theresa quipped.

It was Jenny, barely discernable over the wail of a newborn. "Hey, Miriam, guess what?"

"Um, you had your baby?"

"Lauren Emily. Seven pounds, five ounces, twenty-one inches long. Can you believe it?"

"Congratulations," Miriam said, emptying the freezer of all the foil-wrapped food still left from the funeral. It felt good to throw it all away. "How'd labor go?"

"You will NOT believe how painful it is. How come no one warns us ahead of time? It was eight and a half hours of absolute torture because everything moved so fast they couldn't give me an epidural. I felt it all, the ripping, and the stitching, even though the doctor gave me a local."

"Yikes."

"But," Jenny's voice softened into a sing-song, "here she is, and she's so beautiful!"

"Makes it all worth it, huh?"

"Exactly. So have you finished your childbirth class yet?"

"I'm supposed to tour the maternity ward next week, but I keep putting off the birthing class."

"You'd better do that soon. It actually was helpful, I thought. So what are you up to today?"

"Today's the move. We're packing up the truck right now."

"I won't keep you, then. Hold on, let me grab a pen so you can give me your new number."

"No need. I got a cell phone from a company that let me keep my old phone number."

"Oh, okay. Oops, the nurse just came in. It's time to try breast-feeding again if I can wake up little Lauren."

Miriam set the phone on the counter and moved to help Theresa with the plates.

"You haven't taken your class yet?" Theresa asked.

"No."

"Why not?"

"I think knowledge is highly overrated. Denial, on the other hand . . ."

"Seriously," Theresa persisted.

"Okay, seriously. I've thought about going a million times. But I feel stupid going by myself."

"Nonsense. You don't go to those classes to prove anything to anyone or to make friends, but to learn how to have a baby."

"They didn't have Lamaze or anything like that when I had children," Mrs. Harmel offered.

"See? And you did just fine, didn't you?"

"Actually, for the first one they knocked me out and used forceps to rip 'er out. I couldn't walk for ten days."

"Oh, God," Miriam groaned. "You are both evil."

"I'll go to Lamaze or whatever it's called with you," offered Ben, who had come into the room carrying a box from the basement.

"You can't go with her," Theresa said. "That's gross."

Miriam laughed. "Please tell me that's the last box downstairs."

"You wish," he said, dumping the carton and grabbing a Mountain Dew before heading toward the stairs again.

Miriam was glad when the conversation turned to other topics.

With only a few more boxes to load and last-minute vacuuming to do, Miriam left to sign papers and hand over the keys. Afterward, she would meet them all at the new house, where Joseph would be arriving with lunch. The men especially looked like they needed a break, with their t-shirts sticking to them like a second skin.

It was a singularly lonely experience, signing her name over and over again on the line with enough space for two signatures. To honor Paul, she at first tried to read all the fine print but soon gave up. "Just tell me where to sign," she told the lawyer, and it was over quickly.

Driving up to the new house, she felt a jolt upon seeing Paul's Miata parked against the curb. Ben had driven it over with the top down, Miriam's ficus tree sprouting from the passenger seat. She had become accustomed to ignoring it in the garage, but here, its sleek silver presence was painfully out of context.

Theresa was sitting on the front steps, and all the men were sprawled on the grass. Figment complained hoarsely from his carrier on the porch.

"I leave for an hour and you guys think its time to work on your tans?" she called to them.

"Very funny," Steven said.

Letting herself into the house, she found the air inside stifling. She hadn't thought it would be necessary to ask the previous owners to leave the air-conditioning on.

Theresa followed her into the kitchen, where it was immediately apparent that no cleaning had been done. The floor was filthy, and a quick glance in the cupboards revealed crumbs and dirt.

"Apparently their arms were broken and they were struck blind," Theresa said, looking in the freezer, where a bag of peas had spilled open, leaving green pebbles stuck in little mounds.

"Let's eat lunch outside," Miriam suggested, her voice echoing through the empty rooms, "and give the air a chance to catch up."

Joseph had arrived with sandwiches and was already handing them out. He had also brought a few lawn chairs and helped Miriam get situated in one of them under the shade of a maple tree, bringing her a sandwich and a bottle of ice-cold water dripping with condensation. His solicitousness embarrassed her.

"Have you figured out what you're doing this summer after your trip to Scotland?" Steven asked Ben.

"Yeah, I'm going to keep working for my history professor. He's writing a book on the Rurikov Dynasty. He wants me to help him do research."

"Rurikov? Who or what was that?" Joseph wanted to know.

"The Rurikov Dynasty ruled Russia from 859 to 1240 A.D. You've probably heard of Alexander Nevsky? He was a descendent of Rurikov. Professor Lynch said he'd let me co-write the chapter on medieval weaponry."

Carl slapped him on the back, and even Theresa looked pleased.

"You should talk to my friend Svetlana," Miriam said, swallowing a bite of turkey sandwich. "She's from Russia, and I have a feeling she knows a lot about her country's history. Ask her one question and she'll go on and on."

"It's true," Steven laughed. "I helped Miriam take some furniture over to Svetlana's apartment and made the mistake of admitting that I had never read Dostoevsky."

"She was horrified," Miriam laughed.

"'The best author in entire world,'" Steven imitated Svetlana's heavy accent, "'and you've never read his books?' She gave me a lecture on the greatest writers in the world, who are all, of course, Russian. I have to read *The Brothers Karamazov* and report back to her."

"She'll hold you to it," Miriam said.

"How do you know her?" Theresa asked.

"She was one of Paul's clients. She didn't have a single piece of furniture, so I gave her some of the stuff I didn't need anymore."

"That was awfully generous," Theresa said, in a tone that made it clear this was not a compliment.

"She's had a difficult time and it was good to be able to help her out."

"Was that wise, though? I don't think people truly appreciate things unless they've had to work for them. They start thinking they're entitled to handouts."

"Svetlana is working really hard to make it on her own, so I don't think that's an issue. Do you, Steven?"

He didn't answer, as he was engrossed in conversation with Joseph.

Theresa waved a fly away from the plum she had bitten into and started to say something, but Ben interrupted her. "Mom, have you ever met Svetlana?"

"No."

"Then shut up about it."

Carl, who was lying on his back, raised his head to look at his son, then lowered it again and closed his eyes.

Theresa took another bite, chewing furiously. Mouth full, she said, "I was just trying to protect you, Miriam, because you can be naïve sometimes."

Miriam raised her eyebrows at Ben, who shrugged. She had to hide a smile, which felt surprising and new.

"All right, crew," Steven said, clapping his hands and stretching. "Enough lounging. Let's get back to work."

The truck was emptied relatively quickly, and when they no longer needed to go in and out of the house so frequently, Miriam let Figment out of his cage. He showed his appreciation by biting her ankle before tearing from room to room, leaping on and off furniture and boxes, until finally settling on the fireplace mantel, where he arched his back whenever anyone walked near him.

Although she tried to tell everyone to go home, no one would hear of leaving.

"Really," she insisted. "I was planning to unpack slowly over the next few weeks."

"We'd rather you spent the next few weeks trying to figure out where we put things," Carl said, as everyone scattered to different rooms.

Whether it was the heat or the constant physical labor, Miriam began to feel slightly sick, though she tried hard not to show it. She and Theresa worked in the kitchen together, scrubbing cabinets and washing newsprint from the dishes. Without asking, Theresa began stacking glasses in a cupboard near the stove.

"I'd rather have those over here," Miriam said, indicating a shelf close to the sink.

"But over here they'll be closer to the table, which will make it easier to set."

Miriam started to shrug in agreement, but stopped herself. Why was she such a pushover? "But over here, they'll be closer to the dishwasher," she said, "which will make them easier to put away."

Without speaking, Theresa moved the cups where Miriam wanted them. When she finished, she began putting away the plates, again without asking.

"Over here," Miriam corrected her choice of cupboard, annoyed when Theresa again protested.

Where she wanted the dishes was not a moral issue, to be sure, and she felt slightly ridiculous to be arguing over something so trivial, but she forced herself to not fall back into the old pattern of thoughtlessly acquiescing just to make Theresa happy. Miriam could only hope that with practice, it would get easier. More than facing Theresa, or anyone else for that matter, as the sometimes opponent that she was, it was hard doing battle with herself, with her habitual way of relating. Like using muscles that had been dormant her entire life.

"Silverware, pots and pans, serving dishes," Miriam pointed to drawers and shelves, naming the arrangement of the entire kitchen.

"Okay, okay," Theresa said, raising her hands defensively.

They worked for a while in silence, hearing the occasional yell and thump from the men as they knocked furniture against the walls.

Miriam leaned against the counter, grimacing.

"You okay?"

"Just a small contraction," Miriam said, massaging her tight stomach. The doctor had told her to expect these little spasms of muscle that made her breath hitch and then were gone in the time it took to exhale. "I'm okay." She put her hands back in the soapy water to wash another plate.

"You should rest."

"No, I'm good."

"There's no sense in pushing yourself so hard you get sick. Come with me."

Miriam reluctantly followed her upstairs, where Theresa showed her that the bed had been set up and made with clean linen.

"I want you to sleep for at least an hour. Don't even think about getting up and doing anything until then."

"Aye, aye, captain," Miriam said, grinning. Her whole body ached. Back, hips, arms, legs. She knew that no matter the depth of her exhaustion, the combination of knowing the others were still working and the restlessness of the baby whenever she stopped moving would ensure she wouldn't sleep.

"If you guys want to go home—"

"Don't be silly." Theresa pulled the shades and twiddled her fingers on the way out of the room.

Strange and a little unsettling to see her own bed in a different room. She heard her sister's voice through the wall, where Carl was assembling the crib. Carl's reply was a soft murmur.

Miriam dug through a few boxes until she found her baby name book. She had worked her way through the Gs, so far finding nothing that she liked. Farrell, Fergus, Frank . . . ugh. There had to be something better than Henry Paul, a suggestion made by her father-in-law.

When she lay down, she felt something hard jutting into her thigh. She dug in her pocket, pulling out the rock. The new room felt more like home once she had returned it to its spot on the bedside table.

Music blasted through the house and was silenced. "Sorry," Ben yelled from the living room. He must be hooking up the surround-sound system.

She smiled and turned the page.

After pizza and beer and a lot of good-natured groaning about the amount of stuff Miriam owned, everyone hugged her good-bye.

On his way out, Ben dug in his pocket for the keys to the Miata. "Before I forget," he said, holding them out to her.

She closed his fingers around them. "Actually, it's yours now," she said.

He stared at her.

"The title and all the papers are in the glove compartment. I already signed them over to you."

"No way," he said, trying to force the keys into her hand.

"What am I going to do, take the baby out for a joy ride on Friday nights?"

He looked embarrassed with indecision. "I don't know what to say."

She pulled him into a hug. "Paul would have wanted it," she whispered, and he squeezed her in response.

# twenty-one

*a*t the hospital entrance, Steven switched off the engine,

but before he could get around the car to help Miriam out,

an elderly man wearing a purple vest and volunteer pin opened her door and held out a hand. The August heat rolled in so heavy with moisture it was difficult to breathe. When she didn't move, the man asked, "Are you having a pain, my dear?"

She nodded, staring at the dust that filled the crevices of the dashboard while she waited for the clamp around her midsection to let up.

The volunteer drummed his fingers on the roof of the car in a rhythmic, though not impatient pattern and whistled tunelessly through his front teeth.

"Okay," she said when it was over, and he helped her into a wheelchair. He stopped before the entrance and started to turn her toward the parking lot, as if to wait for Steven to catch up to them.

"I'm going to have a heat stroke out here," she said sharply.

"Oh, of course," he said cheerfully. "Don't know what I was thinking." He pushed her inside and stopped near the information desk, where a fan with yellow crepe paper tied to its face oscillated back and forth.

Miriam fanned herself with both hands, wanting to kick herself for being impatient with the first person to cross her path. The volunteer had taken up his tune again, and she took this as a sign that he wasn't offended. "No one expects you to be perfect," Paul had told her once. "Except me. When you're cooking my dinner."

When Steven appeared three contractions later through the revolving door, bag in hand, the volunteer patted her shoulder and said, "Here comes Dad, now. You'll be fine."

She started to correct him but realized Steven's presence would prevent others from knowing how alone she truly was. That her grief could thus be held private was a small comfort.

The pains, as he so quaintly put it, had started in the early morning. At three AM she had been awakened by a dream in which a giant rubber band was being stretched tight and snapped against her lower back. Again and again, pain erupted at the point of contact, radiating through her pelvis. When she got up to pace, she rubbed the small of her back with the heel of her hand, surprised when the bedroom mirror didn't reveal a fresh bruise.

She dug Paul's watch out of the bedside table and curled up in bed, pushing the button that illuminated the face and anxiously watching the second hand click its way around the dial. There was no discernable pattern to the contractions yet. Forty seconds of pain, then three minutes of nothing. Sixty seconds, then a fifteen-minute lull. Sometimes she would be on the verge of dozing when the rubber band would yank her back to reality. The watch cast a faint green glow onto her white sheets.

Light was beginning to peek through the curtains when she got up to wash the sheen of sweat off her face. As she headed back to bed, her legs buckled, and she found herself on the floor, where a contraction rocked her back and forth. She had known it would hurt, but my God. She had no idea what she was doing. Why hadn't she gone to a childbirth class? Because now she was in trouble. *Why didn't I suck it up and just go?* When her muscles relaxed and she was able to crawl, she made her way to the telephone and dialed her brother.

"I'll be right over," Steven said as soon as he heard her tight voice.

He must have run the entire way, because he arrived before the next contraction hit, hair sticking up every which way and pillow marks on his cheek. Even though it was only four houses away, he was breathing with effort. She had made it only halfway down the stairs, trailing a hastily packed overnight bag.

"Steven," she gasped, "I didn't take any classes and I haven't packed or read any books or watched any videos. I bought finger puppets and a dozen socks, of all things, but not a car seat—"

He made shushing noises and helped her down the remainder of the stairs, steering her toward the front door.

"What am I going to do? I don't know how I'm going to do this—"

"Women have been having babies for thousands of years without modern medicine—"

"Yeah, and a lot of them died." A contraction redirected her. "The couch, the couch," she cried, and they doubled back so she could collapse on the soft cushions. Her stomach churned.

"I need a bowl," she breathed between gritted teeth.

"A bowl?" Steven said, confused. "What for?"

*Paul would have known.* "A bowl. A plastic bag. A garbage can. I don't care. In case I puke."

Steven scrambled into the kitchen, where she heard him banging through cupboards and drawers. Something big crashed to the floor and she could only hope it wasn't her brother, passed out. The contraction subsided, taking with it the urge to throw up, so when he ran back into the room lugging her biggest bowl, an extremely heavy, oversized porcelain mixing bowl, and realized—she could see it in his expression—that there was no room on her lap for such a monstrosity, she started laughing.

"Where'd you get that?" she asked.

He looked at the bowl as though seeing it for the first time. "I don't know." He turned it slowly in his hands. "I think the cupboard above the refrigerator."

The place for items she rarely used. The thought of him standing on tiptoes, digging through the most out-of-the-way, difficult-to-reach cupboard, was hilarious. With so many other options available to him, *this* is what he had grabbed. She howled.

"Well," he said, a sheepish grin spreading over his face.

"In the pantry beside the refrigerator," she directed, wiping her eyes, "is a canvas holder stuffed full of plastic bags. A couple of those would be fine."

This time there were no frantic noises or crashes from the kitchen. Miriam breathed in as deeply as she could and let the air out slowly, rubbing her already sore stomach muscles. She needed to get a grip. Their little comedy of errors had helped break her panic; she found herself thinking more clearly now. How would Paul reason this out? Her water hadn't broken yet, so there wasn't an urgent need to get to the hospital—besides which she hated doctors and would rather be at home as long as she could. First babies often took a long time and she had been in labor for what, five hours, tops? It felt like days. Oh, she was in for it.

She called her doctor, who confirmed she could wait at home until the contractions got closer together and were consistently one to two minutes in duration. Steven didn't want to leave her, so she settled on the couch while he carefully timed her labor, making notations on a scrap of paper. Every once in a while she would think of something else she wanted to take to the hospital and would send Steven upstairs to retrieve it, and so they passed a few hours together in near silence.

"My wallet," she said. "Up in the drawer of the bedside table in my room. It's leather—you'll see it. Should be right on top." *My* wallet, she called it, but really it was Paul's, and if Steven flipped it open or wondered why she wanted his wallet, he didn't say anything. The next time he stepped out of the room to get a glass of water for himself, she slipped Paul's driver's license out of its slot and pushed the wallet under the couch. They had always laughed at his picture, which the clerk had taken without warning. Eyes half closed, mouth turned down and slightly open, shadows on his face that made his cheeks look sunken, skin a yellowish hue. He looked like a stoned convict. All that was missing was a plaque with numbers in front of his chest. She didn't look at the picture or smile thinking of it, just covered his face with her thumb and held it tight, feeling the plastic grow warm in her hands.

Mid-afternoon her water broke, and with great calm, they headed to the hospital. It took only a few minutes in the hospital room for Miriam to be glad she had labored at home as long as she did. She was stripped of her clothes and wrapped in a flimsy gown; a nurse named Chrissie with too-blonde hair and long, painted nails took her temperature and raised her eyebrows when Miriam said Steven was her brother, not the father. She wouldn't have bothered explaining, except that when Chrissie examined her, Steven stepped out of the room and the nurse remarked on his unusual modesty.

"Is the father going to be here?" Chrissie asked, as though she had a right to know.

"No."

"Is he away on business?"

"No."

"Ah ha," she said, insinuatingly.

"Actually, my husband died in December."

"Wow. That's awful."

Chrissie started an IV and placed a monitor on Miriam's belly, wrapping its straps tightly around her back, and though the steady sound of the baby's heartbeat was comforting, the pressure, like a second rubber band, made her back ache in a new way.

Although her doctor had instructed her to have the hospital call him when she arrived, once she met the doctor on duty, she told them not to bother. Dr. Felix was an extremely short, though stocky man with a warm handshake and a shocking amount of curly brown hair. He fairly crackled with energy, rubbing his hands together as though he could hardly stand the anticipation before examining her.

"How long have you been in labor?" he asked as he snapped off the surgical gloves and reached for the chart.

"Since three this morning."

"Ah, four lousy centimeters after all these hours," he said sympathetically. He sat in the chair by the bed and leaned toward her as if he had all the time in the world. "You're doing all right?"

"I think, yes," she said, embarrassed because her eyes had teared up at his tenderness.

He nodded thoughtfully, eyes still searching her face. "I predict you're going to handle this just fine. Right now all you can do is let the contractions work their magic. Keep reminding yourself that you're almost halfway there."

After he left, Chrissie and a medical student both wanted to gauge her progress, making her regret choosing a teaching hospital. The medical student obviously didn't know what he was doing and groped around for so long she nearly screamed in frustration.

Through all this activity, Miriam had suffered a mere three contractions, and each time Chrissie looked at the monitor and made declarations like: "That was hardly strong enough to be a real contraction." Miriam knew better than to try to explain that being at the hospital had broken the rhythm of labor she had been in all morning. "Believe me," Chrissie said as she left the room, "they're going to have to get a lot stronger before you'll be able to get this baby out."

Steven had returned with a cup of coffee by this time, looking as though he had found a mirror. His hair was slightly damp and smoothed down. "The nurse is an idiot, isn't she?" he observed.

"You don't know the half of it. You'll forgive me if I say or do something unforgivable, won't you?"

"Of course."

"It's like I can't control my emotions—every time she says something to me, I want to put her in a headlock."

He watched her over the rim of the coffee cup, his eyes amused.

"And that medical student, I swear I nearly kicked him in the face. Boom, kick. He'd never know what hit him."

Steven laughed.

"You think I'm kidding?"

He shook his head. "No, I believe you. But if you do kick someone, please wait until I'm in the room. I want to witness it."

She watched him examine the long sheets of graph paper rolling from the machine next to her bed.

"That coffee smells wonderful," she said.

"This? You want some?"

"No, it just smells good for some reason."

"The nurse showed me where to get ice and juice, so I can get some whenever you want. There's grape, apple, and orange juice. And water, of course."

"Steven, will you stay the whole time? That is, if it doesn't make you uncomfortable."

"*I'm* fine. But I was going to say that if *you* would feel more comfortable having a woman here, I'd understand."

"Like who, Theresa?" She made a face thinking of her sister trying to boss her through labor. "There's no one else I'd want here."

"Then there's no place I'd rather be."

The muscles in her belly clamped down, and she allowed the sensation to carry her away, relaxing into the pain, riding the wave like a kayaker going through rapids. For once her physical and emotional states were echoes of one another; it felt right to be in this exact spot.

"Don't forget to breathe," Steven said quietly.

She nodded, eyes closed.

When she opened her eyes, Steven was watching her intently. "That was a big one," he said, pointing to the graph. "Look how high it got."

"It must be a guy thing. Paul would be fascinated by that, too."

"I'm sorry he's missing this," Steven replied.

They fell quiet, listening to the noises of the hospital. The nurses' station was down the hall, but she could hear their chatter—not the exact words, but the lilt of normal, everyday gossip and conversation. Laughter, even. Every few minutes a doctor was paged in the hallway, and was that . . . a contraction turned Miriam's attention inward . . . but not before she confirmed: Yes, it was a woman screaming.

"Could you shut the door?" she asked, remembering this time to breathe.

"They're getting longer, too," Steven said, stroking the hair at her temple until her body was released.

When her eyes refocused, she could tell he wanted to ask her a question. "What?"

"I was just wondering about Esther. I sort of thought she might be here."

"I couldn't ask her to be here."

"How come?"

"She had another miscarriage."

"What's that got to do with you?"

"I know, but I can understand why it would be too painful for her to be around me."

"I don't. It seems to me that good friends get past junk like that."

"I've tried. I've left messages, but she never returns my calls. After a while, I felt like I was stalking her or something. It kills me to know that every time I call her cell, she looks to see who it is and then lets it go to voicemail. I feel like I failed her."

Steven got up and walked to the window. He sipped his coffee a few times. Without turning around, he said, "I think it's the other way around."

Chrissie's sing-song preceded her purple scrub-clad body into the room. "How are we doing in here?" She examined a few feet of ticker tape, rolling it tightly and fastening it with a rubber band. "Hmmmm?" she asked, loudly, and Miriam realized she actually expected an answer.

"Oh. Fine, I think."

"Well, we need your contractions to get more regular before you're going to make much progress." She turned toward Miriam and stood with her hands on her hips. "Just concentrate on letting them do their job. Looks like the baby is doing fine, too. The heartbeat is good and strong."

Miriam was glad the nurse didn't stay in the room for long.

By the time the sky outside had darkened and Steven pulled the curtains, she had only progressed to five centimeters. She threw up the orange juice she had been sipping throughout the day, grateful for the diversion from the merciless rubber band.

She was on her side and Steven was rubbing her lower back. "Steven?"

"Right here, darling," he reassured.

"Why didn't you tell me you were HIV positive?"

His hands stilled for a moment. "I don't know."

"Come here." She directed him to the chair, waited until he sat down. "You were afraid of how I'd react."

He smiled ruefully, looked down at his clasped hands.

"I think—" A contraction took her.

When it subsided, Steven rinsed a washcloth in cold water and gave it to her. She held it against her face and sucked on it just to feel the moisture against her cracked lips.

"I think our roles are going to be reversed at some point in the coming years," she continued. "Hopefully not soon, but sometime."

He looked pained.

"But I want it to be more than that. More than just a role reversal. You've always taken care of me, my whole life. You are the father and mother I never had, even when Mom and Dad were still alive. But now I want . . ." she searched for what she really wanted. "I want us to be friends. Honest with each other. And on equal terms. Not simply caretakers."

He nodded, speechless and not quite meeting her eyes.

Merciless, these contractions. Pushing her under with barely a chance to breathe. "As much as I hate to see her," she groaned, "could you get Chrissie? I'd like her to check me again."

While she was alone in the room, she clutched Paul's driver's license, which she had hidden beneath her pillow, and felt it digging into her palm as she worked her way through another contraction.

When Steven returned, he brought with him a new nurse. There had been a changing of the guard. Laura had a quietness about her that Miriam immediately trusted. Her voice didn't have that condescending edge to it, and her fingernails were mercifully short. She didn't react when Steven admitted he was the "soon-to-be uncle," and she didn't ask where the father was. Miriam felt a great surge of love for her.

Modesty seemed pointless to Miriam by now, and Steven seemed to sense that; he no longer left the room when she was examined.

"You're getting closer," Laura said. "Six and a half centimeters. I know you've been at this for a long time. Your other nurse asked if you wanted an epidural, right?"

"Only a million times."

"And you don't?"

"No."

"Okay. I won't ask again, so if you change your mind, let me know."

"Is Dr. Felix still here?" Miriam asked, suddenly afraid he might've gone home, too. She may have used up all her luck in getting a better nurse.

"No, he'll stay until you're done. He's just finishing up a c-section next door, and hopefully by the time he puts in the last stitch, he'll be needed in here. I'd love to see you have this baby soon."

Laura's kind voice and gentle touch gave Miriam courage. Okay. She could do this.

Several times she asked Steven to peek through the curtains to see if it was getting light out, even though it was only three AM and she was stalled at six and a half centimeters, a full twenty-four hours since she started. She was beyond exhausted. Dazed. A little incoherent. After a particularly strong contraction, her vision cleared, and she saw fear in Steven's eyes. She started to say something reassuring to him, but dozed off instead. Seconds later she was awakened by another contraction.

"How do you feel about taking something to manage the pain?" Laura asked. "There are a number of less invasive options than an epidural, like Nubaine, which can take the edge off the contractions. Give you a little break."

"No." Miriam was too tired to explain, but she needed to feel everything.

"Dr. Felix is a little concerned with how long this is taking. At some point we might need to give you Pitocin to get you over this hump so your contractions actually get you closer to the goal."

"I've heard really bad things about that drug." Miriam remembered when Esther was given Pitocin, the labor had taken a hard turn, and Mei's heartbeats had become irregular.

"It's not our first choice," Laura acknowledged. "But it does have its place. Another option would be a shot of morphine."

"Morphine?" Steven was incredulous. "You can give that to pregnant women?"

"Amazing, huh?" Laura said.

"No," Miriam said wearily. "No pain medication."

"The funny thing about morphine in this context is that it doesn't really work as a pain med. For some reason, it usually has one of two effects. First, it can relax you to the point where you get some sleep, which will allow you to gather your energy for pushing. The longer your labor is, the more beneficial this small reprieve can be. I'd hate to see you get to the pushing stage having already used up every ounce of your strength and energy. The second possibility is that it will actually jump start your contractions so you dilate fully and get to push sooner. Morphine. It's a beautiful thing. Even though we don't completely understand why it works the way it does. And it won't harm the baby."

Miriam looked at Steven—poor, tired Steven—who said, "It's up to you."

"You'd recommend it?" she asked Laura.

"I think it's worth a try."

"How long do you think I'll have to push?"

"It's hard to say. Some women only push a few times, but others have to go at it for a few hours. Maybe you're getting the hard part out of the way and the pushing will go quickly for you. You never know."

The way Laura talked to her as though she were a human being and an adult made her agree. "Okay. Let's do it."

When the nurse left to get the medicine, Miriam took Steven's hand. "Why don't you go lie down in the lounge for a few hours? You look like you could use the sleep as much as me."

"No, I don't want to leave you alone."

"I'm not alone," she said without thinking, and as soon as the words were out, she knew it was true. She didn't feel alone. "Really, Steven. I'd feel better if you got some sleep. Please."

"Let me get some ice for you first. And promise that if you need me, you'll have Laura come get me."

"Cross my heart."

The morphine, as Laura had said, sent Miriam into a light but blessed sleep. She had watched the nurse insert the needle into the IV, felt a slight tingling where the needle was taped to her arm, and then, twilight. In the distance, a rubber band twanged, but it was a sound more than a sensation and easily ignored.

Miriam felt someone at her side and opened her eyes with an effort—the nurse had dimmed the lights and left the room—and there was Paul, leaning over the side rails of the hospital bed, pressing his ear against her belly, the tips of his fingers creating ten gentle pressure points on her tired muscles. He was humming a song that sounded so familiar it ached in her veins, a lullaby whose quiet tones were both melancholy and comforting at the same time. Then he lifted her gown and pressed his lips against her bare skin. He used her belly button as an intercom—she grinned in recognition, for this is something he would do—*my little baby girl, you are so lucky. You have the best mom in the world.* He turned his head and made eye contact with Miriam, his beautiful eyes getting lost in crinkles.

As if shot with adrenaline, Miriam knew instinctively that her labor had changed, that it was almost time. How long she had slept, she had no idea—minutes, seconds, hours?—and she worked through several contractions, breathing short puffs of air, embarrassing herself with noises that weren't quite human. Needing to push more than anything she'd ever before needed, she fumbled for the intercom.

Laura's voice crackled with static as she said simply, "Coming."

"I need to push," Miriam pleaded the moment she was in the room, hardly able to stand the wait while Laura examined her.

"Holy smokes, you've really gone to town," the nurse exclaimed. "And I only gave you the morphine two hours ago."

"You'd better get Steven," she said through clenched teeth.

The room began to bustle with activity. Laura rolled a clear-plastic bassinet close to the bed, directed Miriam's heels into the stirrups, and whipped out a tray of instruments for the doctor, who settled himself on a stool between her legs. Laura coached Steven to count to ten each time Miriam pushed so she'd know how long to bear down. During the intervals, he rubbed a piece of ice over her lips.

"You're doing great, Mrs. Kovatch," Dr. Felix cheered her on. "You're almost there, I promise."

"Can you see the head?" Miriam asked Steven.

"Can he see the head?" Dr. Felix exclaimed. "He can see practically the entire baby! Just give me a few more pushes . . . that's right, really good . . ." And he joined in the counting.

Over with. She just wanted it over with. And suddenly it was. A great surge, and her body was once again completely her own. In the cessation of contractions, she felt her aloneness, but only for the second it took the baby to gasp and let out a wail.

"It's a girl!" Dr. Felix shouted, hoisting the little body in the air like a trophy before placing her on Miriam's slack belly.

"It's you," Miriam said, touching the warm, living skin, the wet hair, feeling as if she had known this little body forever. The baby's fists punched wildly at the air as the nurse toweled her off.

"But I thought you were going to be a boy," Miriam said, laughing when the crunched-up face turned toward her voice. The baby's lower lip quivered, and her eyebrows were deeply furrowed above her blinking eyes. "Look, Steven, it's your niece."

"What's her name?" Laura asked.

"Her name? I don't know! The ultrasound person told me it was going to be a boy, so I only had boys' names picked out."

Dr. Felix rolled his eyes. "Ultrasound techs," he said under his breath.

"Don't worry about it. You've got seven days before we have to complete the birth certificate."

"You want to do the honors?" Dr. Felix asked Steven, holding out a pair of scissors.

Steven wiped his eyes with the back of his hand and looked at Miriam.

She nodded.

So Steven cut the cord, and Miriam remembered Paul's words as he spoke into her belly button. *My little baby girl,* he had said. "Your daddy knew," she murmured to the eyes that were still searching her face. "He knew all along."

## twenty-two

*a*s Steven leaned over the hospital bed to get one last look at the baby before going home to shower and change clothes, Miriam noticed with a sharp feeling of guilt how haggard he looked. Deep bluish marks beneath his eyes, stubble covering the angular lines of his cheekbones and jaw. She made him promise to stay at home and sleep rather than hurrying back.

Though exhausted, she felt too wired to sleep herself. She made calls instead.

To her surprise, Henry picked up the phone while she was leaving a message on their answering machine.

"Congratulations, Grandpa," she said, and as if on cue, the baby stretched her body against the cocoon of blankets and squeaked in protest—a sound she knew would carry over the phone. Henry didn't say anything, but neither did he hang up, so she plowed ahead.

"Your granddaughter was born at five this morning, six pounds five ounces, twenty inches long. She's perfect. With tons of curly hair. I don't have a name yet." She waited for a response. Nothing. Not even breathing. She wondered where Martha was and why she hadn't picked up the extension. "Well, I guess that's all I have to say. I'll send pictures as soon as I get some developed and I'll call when—"

"We've already got plane tickets for two weeks from Friday," he said, gruffly. "Have Steven pick us up at 3:21, same airline as always." The line clicked off.

"Okay," she said, feeling a trill of anxiety in the pit of her stomach, but surprisingly, no anger. It was right for them to come visit. Only after she hung up did she realize that Henry had ignored her request that he check with her before making travel plans. And that he had already planned to come, whether the baby was a boy or a girl.

A new nurse arrived to help her attempt breast-feeding again. The baby was so groggy, it was hard to get her interested. They stroked her cheek, tapped her chin, took off all her clothes and changed her diaper, which she didn't like and made her squall. When Miriam finally managed to get the baby latched on, the tenderness of her nipple made her toes curl.

"Yow," she said, and the nurse laughed.

Theresa was the first visitor to come bursting into the room, crying, "Where's my niece?"

"She needs to be burped," Miriam said, handing her over.

"Oh, would you look at her?" Theresa dropped her packages and cradled the baby against her shoulder gently, bouncing from one foot to the other, patting her back and urging her to burp. "Get the bubbles out of your itsy bitsy tummy," she cooed.

It cracked Miriam up to hear her normally gruff sister talking like this.

"Here, I brought you some things." Theresa scooped the packages off the floor and dumped them on the bed.

There were carefully wrapped packages of receiving blankets, dresses, and socks with lace sewn on the edges, a stuffed elephant, and rattles that could be Velcroed around little wrists. All pink. Even the elephant.

"How did you know she was going to be a girl?"

"I didn't. I bought two of everything, one set in blue, one in pink. I'll take the blue stuff back."

"Thanks, Theresa. It's all so . . ." she paused, thinking: *pink.* "Beautiful."

"Anything for you, my cute little baby," Theresa murmured into the baby's ear, still swaying and dancing around the room. "She needs a name, Miriam," she demanded.

"I know." Miriam punched one of her pillows trying to get comfortable, only half-listening to Theresa's scolding. "I'm so tired I actually feel sick to my stomach," she confessed.

"Yeah, childbirth will do that to you. But you'll feel better soon." Theresa placed the baby in the bassinet. "As much as I hate to, I should go so you can sleep. You want me to send the baby to the nursery?"

Miriam shook her head. "She's okay here."

Theresa looked as though she wanted to touch Miriam, hug her or kiss her on the cheek or touch her arm. But she didn't. She just stood at the end of the bed with a little smile on her face. Then was gone.

Even though every cell in her body was slack and used up, all Miriam could manage was a light slumber, interrupted every time a new noise issued from the bassinet. Eventually she gave up and moved to the edge of the bed, where she could watch her daughter's eyes flutter beneath translucent eyelids.

"You make beautiful babies," she whispered, and sensed Paul knew it.

There was a gentle knocking on the door. "Hello?" a voice called out. It was Esther. "Are you in there?"

"Come in," she said, shocked. Mei appeared, toting a bunch of brightly colored balloons with Esther right behind.

"Look, we brought balloons, where's the baby?" Mei blurted, standing on tiptoe to try to see into the bassinet.

"She's right here." Miriam picked up the baby and motioned for Esther to lift Mei up onto the bed next to her.

"Are you going to feed her?" Mei wanted to know.

"No, she ate a few minutes ago, so she's ready to sleep for a while."

Mei shook her head in adult wonder. "She is so beautiful," she breathed.

"Breast-feeding. It hurts like anything, doesn't it?" Esther said. "In our birthing class, the instructor said that while you're pregnant, you should toughen up your nipples by having your spouse rub them between his fingers. Charles thought that was a great idea, of course. But he tried it once and I nearly killed him. Told him I *would* kill him if he ever did it again."

Miriam laughed. "Please tell me it gets easier."

"Yeah. By the time the baby's six weeks old, it'll be a piece of cake."

"Six weeks? Oh, man."

"It'll go fast. Trust me."

Miriam unwrapped the baby's clothes to show off the little body. It was a good excuse; she couldn't seem to get enough of the sight of her daughter. Mei was fascinated by the bellybutton. She rewrapped the blanket and handed her over to Esther, who expertly tucked the little bundle into the crook of her arm.

"Look at all this hair," she said, touching the curls. "And eyebrows! Babies don't usually have eyebrows, but you are just gorgeous." She brushed her lips against the downy forehead, and Miriam realized she had been waiting for a gesture just like this—something to tell her that Esther didn't hold her daughter's existence against her.

"What's her name?"

"She doesn't have one."

Esther looked at Miriam for a beat and then laughed. "Oh, boy," she said. In a baby voice, she asked, "What did Theresa say about that, I wonder?"

Oh, she had missed her friend, who knew her so well. "It's driving her crazy. 'What do you mean you don't have a name yet?'" Miriam mimicked. "'You've had nine months to figure it out. Name her Jean.'"

"She said that?"

"Jean was my mother's middle name. I was surprised."

"That Theresa would have the audacity to name your daughter for you? It sounds just like her."

"No, that she would choose our mother's name since they never got along."

"Maybe she feels guilty that she was such a lousy daughter herself and doesn't have a way to make it up now."

"Theresa? Feel guilty about something? She's the only Catholic in the world who was spared."

"I just can't believe all this hair," Esther exclaimed again, shaking her head.

Mei got down from the bed and jumped up and down. "Can I hold her, please, Mommy?"

Miriam motioned that it was fine with her. Esther had the little girl sit cross-legged in the chair and then showed her how to carefully support the baby's head and body. Mei immediately began rocking back and forth. "Hush little baby, don't say a word," she piped sweetly, her little voice raised in song. "Mama's gonna buy you a diamond ring."

Esther sat down on the bed near Miriam's feet, and they were silent for a while, listening to Mei.

"I'm glad you're here," Miriam said. "But I know it must be painful for you."

Esther started to respond, but Miriam interrupted. "No. I don't want you to pretend that everything's fine when it's not. I don't know what it's like to miscarry, but

I can imagine that it doesn't stop hurting after four months, or however long it's been."

"I have a really hard time being around pregnant women," Esther confessed. "It makes me feel like I've got this blinking sign over my head that says 'defective.' A lot of people think that because I have Mei, the miscarriages shouldn't matter. But it's because I have Mei that I know what I'm missing. Whenever I'm around anyone who's pregnant, I feel awful and left out."

"Even me?"

"Yeah," she nodded, looking ashamed. "I'm sorry."

Mei was now singing, "A you're adorable, B you're so beautiful, C you're a cutie full of cha-arm. . . ."

Miriam couldn't tell if Esther was apologizing for her difficulty with pregnant women or for the way she had lashed out at the birthday party, and realized, with surprise, that it didn't matter.

Esther wrapped her arms around her body, looking miserable. "I'm pregnant," she whispered, obviously not wanting Mei to overhear.

Miriam's heart leapt out of fearful joy for her friend, and something else. "How far along?"

"Six weeks. I am so scared." Her expression was fierce. "If I lose this one . . . I don't know. I don't know if I can go through that again."

Miriam hugged her tight. "I'll pray," she said, meaning it. She would pray. Not only for Esther, but for herself as well. She realized now that if Esther were not pregnant, she might not have come to make amends. Either way, it was Miriam's turn to be the friend Esther needed, to offer whatever small reserves of strength she had stored up.

Early the following morning, while it was still dark outside, the baby woke up crying. Inconsolable. Miriam did everything she could think of—checked her diaper, offered her a breast, twiddled a pacifier between her lips, burped and rocked and jiggled and bounced and walked, but still the crying kept on.

For a while, Miriam found herself humming one of Mei's lullabies, but suddenly a different musical note resonated within her, an elusive tone that had been surfacing from a dream. She tried to relax her mind, hoping the song would allow her to catch up. Another revolution around the room and there . . . she chased forward and caught it.

It was the lullaby Paul sang when he joined her in the delivery room. *Sing sweet and low, a lullaby. Till angels say amen. A little child shall lead them, the prophets said of old. In storm and tempest heal them until the bell is tolled.*

Miriam crawled back onto the bed and stripped the baby of everything except her diaper, unsnapped her own gown and cradled the baby, whose skin was red and clammy from the exertion of crying, against her bare chest.

*Sing sweet and low your lullaby, till angels say amen.*

Snuggled against her, skin to skin, the baby began to calm. Miriam breathed deeply of her scent—warm, new, fresh—and felt fiercely broken, overwhelmed by the depth of love she felt for this wizened, wrinkled face, and deeply afraid for this child who had only her to rely on for safety and wisdom and discipline and everything else children needed. The pain of missing Paul was visceral.

Svetlana called mid-morning, apologizing profusely for not visiting; her car had broken down and she was taking the bus to and from work, but unable to get many other places.

"No problem," Miriam reassured. "Next week, if I'm feeling better, we can come over and visit you."

"Right now you are feeling very bad?"

"No, not too bad. I'm tired. And sore."

"It was long labor?"

"About twenty-six hours. But Steven helped me through it."

"It's good to have family."

"Yes, it is."

"Now let me speak to the baby. She is right there, in your arms?"

"Yes."

"Hold the phone so she can hear."

Curious, Miriam tilted the phone toward the baby. A rapid string of Russian flowed from the receiver, rolling sounds like water flowing over boulders in a stream. It was a beautiful and strange language. After a moment of silence, she brought the receiver back to her mouth.

"What did you say?" she asked.

"Oh, it was just Russian blessing. And now she hears my voice, knows we will meet soon."

Gathering herself to go home, Miriam sent the baby to the nursery so she could shower without worrying about someone sneaking into the room and snatching her. She tried to keep from falling into worry about other things. Like how she'd shower at home or cook or perform any of those other tasks that would require leaving the baby unattended. She guessed she'd just have to let her cry. *Single motherhood stinks,* she thought. She winced at the tenderness of her muscles. Her stomach was wobbly, no longer stretched taut. She hoped that would go away soon. The nurse had said the stretch marks would resolve into thin silvery traces, which she hoped was true. Not that anyone would see her naked anytime soon.

Getting out of the hospital gown and into a skirt and fresh blouse felt good. She could almost believe she was human.

Before the nurse brought the baby back to the room, Miriam reached for her phone and called Bob Carley.

He was surprised to hear her voice, but as he launched into small talk, he seemed to not be holding a grudge over her quitting.

She tried to take courage from this. "The reason I'm calling," she said, "is that I wonder if you would meet me for lunch sometime soon." So he wouldn't get the wrong idea, she explained hastily, "I'm going to apply to an architecture program and was wondering if you would look at some of my sketches, and if you think I've got potential, maybe you could write a recommendation for me."

"I'd be glad to do that. How does next Tuesday sound?"

She practically stammered. "That would be fine."

"See you then," he said, clicking off.

She put the phone back in her purse with trembling fingers. The thought of having him evaluate her designs still terrified her, but she was determined to push through it. Although downsizing her home would make the insurance money last longer, she'd have to go back to work eventually. Perhaps Paul was right, and she could do better than secretary.

She opened the curtains and saw it was dark outside, the sky heavy with threatening clouds. It was clearly only a matter of time before the storm hit.

Steven arrived as the nurse was weighing the baby one last time. In only a diaper and t-shirt with sleeves tucked over her hands to keep her from accidentally scratching herself, she waved her arms and legs in protest.

"We're almost ready to go," Miriam told her brother, hovering near the nurse, anxious to get the baby off the cold scale and practically snatching her out of the nurse's hands.

"She cries with her whole body engaged, doesn't she?" He watched over Miriam's shoulder as she tried to get the flailing arms into the sleeves of a soft yellow sleeper. "I feel like that sometimes, too," he cooed.

She latched the baby into the car seat she had borrowed from the hospital and helped Steven load up a cart with all the flowers and gifts that had accumulated, then settled herself in the wheelchair with the car seat on her lap. The nurse pushed her to a side entrance, where they waited for Steven to bring the car around.

Tired of breathing purified air and looking through windows, she asked to be wheeled outside. The air was thick with humidity and the coming rain, and fragrantly green from freshly cut grass that now lay baking on the ground. Crickets buzzed. A hot sound. Miriam breathed deeply and closed her eyes. The ride from her room through the brightly lit hospital corridors had been long and lonely.

A flash of lightning startled her, and all at once it was raining, the drops tamping down the heat and humidity. The nurse tried to pull her back inside, but she resisted. She threw a blanket over the car seat and held her hand steady over the slumbering face, her fingertips resting lightly on the smooth forehead. The baby jumped at the first boom of thunder, her arms and legs flinging out and folding back instantly. It was a gesture Miriam had experienced often from within.

Is this what Job felt when God restored to him his wealth, gave him new children, cleared his skin of the festering sores that had been only a small straw on the scale of his misery? Nothing could replace the children who had died. Or wipe away the memory of the day when messenger after messenger arrived to describe one more horrifying scene of death and destruction. How long did it take before he could abandon himself to joy?

The baby squirmed as more lightning sizzled above them.

"We'll be home soon," Miriam reassured, lifting her face toward the sky and offering herself up to the drops that wet her face and kept her from knowing if she was crying or not.

Acknowledgments:

Although writing is an inherently solitary profession, I would find it impossible without the help and encouragement of many. This is when I know how blessed I am, when I think about all those who have willingly come alongside me in this process, giving, sometimes sacrificially, of their knowledge, time, and hearts.

My husband combines the best of all worlds; he has an acute mind for business balanced with a love of the arts that makes him clear-headed when I begin to wonder if I wouldn't be better off flipping burgers. Candace Tseng is the best friend a girl could have, aware of my limitations but steadfastly convinced of my ability to make words dance on the page. My parents gave me my start, passing on their love for literature and instilling in me the belief that writing is an honorable profession. I am grateful to my in-laws for their interest and support, and I will never forget that my father-in-law was the very first person to introduce me as a writer. Heather Kennedy, thanks for providing inspiration for the first chapter. Father Jason helped me better understand and appreciate the mystery and yearnings of Catholicism. Larry Tornquist, thank you for hearing me, and in so doing, giving me the courage to believe I have something worth saying.

Abby Frucht, Chris Noël, and Ellen Lesser brought order to the chaos of endless drafts and always seemed to understand what I was aiming for, even before I did. My agent, Britt Carlson, has an infectious enthusiasm that makes me feel like my luck will never run out; I look forward to continuing this journey with her. Gretchen Jaeger's careful editing, deft questions, and amazing insight improved this novel beyond my imaginings. Lil Copan and Paraclete Press, thank you for your commitment to literary fiction, your risk-taking, and for ushering me out of the slush pile.

To all of you, and to those unnamed friends and readers who add spark to my life, my profoundest thanks.

# About Paraclete Press

## Who We Are

Paraclete Press is an ecumenical publisher of books and recordings on Christian spirituality. Our publishing represents a full expression of Christian belief and practice—from Catholic to Evanglical, from Protestant to Orthodox.

Paraclete Press is the publishing arm of the Community of Jesus, an ecumenical monastic community in the Benedictine tradition. As such, we are uniquely positioned in the marketplace without connection to a large corporation and with informal relationships to many branches and denominations of faith.

We like it best when people buy our books from booksellers, our partners in successfully reaching as wide an audience as possible.

## What We Are Doing

### Books

Paraclete Press publishes books that show the richness and depth of what it means to be Christian. Although Benedictine spirituality is at the heart of all that we do, we publish books that reflect the Christian experience across many cultures, time periods, and houses of worship.

We publish books that nourish the vibrant life of the church and its people–books about spiritual practice, formation, history, ideas, and customs.

We have several different series of books within Paraclete Press, including the bestselling *Living Library* series of modernized classic texts; *A Voice from the Monastery*—giving voice to men and women monastics about what it means to live a spiritual life today; award winning literary faith fiction; and books that explore Judaism and Islam and discover how these faiths inform Christian thought and practice.

### Recordings

From Gregorian chant to contemporary American choral works, our music recordings celebrate the richness of sacred choral music through the centuries. Paraclete is proud to distribute the recordings of the internationally acclaimed choir Gloriæ Dei Cantores, who have been praised for their "rapt and fathomless spiritual intensity" by *American Record Guide*, and the Gloriæ Dei Cantores Schola, which specializes in the study and performance of Gregorian chant. Paraclete is also the exclusive North American distributor of the Monastic Choir of St. Peter's Abbey in Solesmes, France, long considered to be a leading authority on Gregorian chant performance.

Learn more about us at our Web site:
www.paracletepress.com, or call us toll-free at
1-800-451-5006.

# More Literary Faith Fiction from Paraclete:

## This Heavy Silence
Nicole Mazzarella

ISBN: 1-55725-425-7
Hardcover
257 pages, $21.95

Strong, resilient, and deeply loyal, Dottie Connell farms her family's three hundred acres in rural Ohio alone, having sacrificed love and family for land she does not even own. A sudden, inexplicable event leaves the daughter of her childhood friend in her care. Spanning a decade, *This Heavy Silence* explores the power of the vows we make to others, and, more binding, those we make to ourselves.

"A novel about family and history, about loneliness and love, about seasons of growth. Ambitious and bittersweet."
—Sheri Reynolds, author of *The Rapture of Canaan,*
**an Oprah Book Selection**

## Life with Strings Attached
Minnie Lamberth

ISBN: 1-55725-416-8
Hardcover
244 pages, $21.95

It is the spring of 1972 in Wellton, Alabama. In the world at large, the Equal Rights Amendment is making its way through the states, the Vietnam War continues, and the Olympics are about to be held in Munich. But for Hannah Hayes, the issues of the world beyond her border pale in comparison to matters more urgent for a seven-year-old—protecting her beagle, Pumpkin, from Ralph, the neighbor's free-spirited dog, and pursuing her dream to become a preacher.

"I just enjoyed the daylights out of this book. Minnie Lamberth's writing reads like the truth, which is the gift of all the best fiction."
—Leif Enger, author of *Peace Like a River*

Available from most booksellers or through Paraclete Press:
www.paracletepress.com; 1-800-451-5006.
*Try your local bookstore first.*